CHAPTER 1

THE NAME IS KETCHELL

The cantina door banged open and Floyd Ketchell stood there with yellow oil light spilling over his face and the Mexican night like a black frame around him.

Faces turned and stared.

Even to the eyes of this gun hell of a border town, he appeared chillingly impressive and possibly lethal in black shirt and blood red bandanna. Some knew him from other times and places he'd drifted through astride his ugly slab-sided horse with a lightning gun riding on his hip. The drinkers here were respectful but not afraid, for they had learned that if left alone, this one would likely in turn leave you be.

Others in the place had read of him in the gaudy Wild West dime novels of the time which ran stories with titles like *Ketchell's Last Bullet* or *Floyd's One-man War!* Some of those yarns were based on actual exploits, others were pure fantasy and fiction. The clients of this border saloon had no way of telling brutal truth from empty newspaper jargon, for the Ketchell they were seeing that night looked capable of just about anything.

Apprehensive yet excited, the patrons of the Tequila Cantina ignored bottles and cards to watch in silence as the newcomer made his light-footed way to the long bar.

To some he was just another dangerous-looking stranger, headed either for the tables, the cells or the undertaker's slab. These were the cynical and the weary, the tired percentage girls, the barman with the high celluloid collar and mutton chop whiskers, the fat and uninterested sheriff, the Mex cardsharks and all the flotsam and jetsam, saints and sinners, of the raw frontier.

For these world-weary and cynical ones, their main interest in the gunfighter was practical. Such as how much money he might be packing, how much trouble he might kick up, whether he might stay on, and if so, for how long.

But whether respectful, wary, uninterested or simply curious, all watched him steadily. These were the faces of the lost souls, too spent and careworn to show much of anything any more. Only one pair of eyes revealed both hate and fear. The man Ketchell had come to kill.

He ordered a John T. Smith rye whiskey and stood rubbing his muscular back against a bar stanchion. He sipped a little, while his green eyes roamed the room, stabbing everywhere except where the tall man in black broadcloth coat stood with his back pressed against a rear wall.

The man's name was Ramon Teel and he was a sidewinder from the Panhandle. Two weeks back he'd taken a shot at a rancher named Mulligan, but had killed the man's wife by mistake. That would prove to be the final shot in the Mulligan-Dewey range war, so the local US marshal had declared, but Floyd Ketchell had corrected the lawman on the spot.

Next-to-last, he'd insisted.

For Ketchell had worked for Mulligan as bodyguard and gunhand over seven violent weeks, long enough to befriend both the rancher and his wife. He was committed to even accounts with the woman-killer when he showed. In the seventh week, Hogue Dewey died from a bad case of lead poisoning so the war was then officially over.

Except for killer Ramon Teel. Teel was still committed to settle an old grudge with Mulligan, regardless of the armistice or death of his enemy's wife. But this plan was thwarted when Ketchell almost caught up with him first. The killer fled but the gunfighter had ruthlessly tracked him over a hundred back-breaking miles to reach this squalid outpost on the banks of the Days of Glory River.

Quickly catching the stink of serious trouble in the air now, the fat sheriff wheezed to his feet and clomped across to confront the newcomer to his town. He met the challenge of cold green eyes and felt the full impact of the gunfighter's powerful personality in just one glance.

The lawman opened his mouth but closed it again. Suddenly talking tough didn't seem such a great idea. So he forced a sick smile and said carefully, 'Er, don't mean to rile you none, stranger, but you should kinda know this here is a peaceful law-abiding town and we'd, you know, kinda like to keep it that way. That's if it's all right with you?'

'It's not.'

The sheriff could take a hint. Pausing only long enough to relieve a drunk of the two fingers of whiskey in his hand, he gulped the spirits down and headed for the exit, some bum clapping derisively as he vanished through the batwings.

Ketchell banged his glass down on the bartop.

'Another John T. Smith!'

The man in the celluloid collar hastily filled the order. Momentarily he wondered if he should maybe warn this young stranger in the black shirt that the tall dude over by the rear door was now furtively working a sneak gun out of his hip pocket. Thinking better of it, he deliberately dropped his bar swab, ducked to retrieve it and failed to reappear.

Ketchell appeared preoccupied with the task of fashioning a quirley. Yet in truth he was as sharply aware of the bartender's disappearance as he had been all along of what was happening over by that rear door.

To a man of his experience such a furtive play as his man was attempting was as clear as large print.

In time a man could get so that he sensed danger even before it raised its head. You learned to distinguish the difference between the furtive rustle of a gopher and the brush of a stalker's boot heel against the grass. These were the skills any man of the gun learned early, or else he died. Ketchell was better at surviving than most.

His apparent inattention was simply part of the lure he was dangling. He doubted Teel would have the guts to face him man to man – gunspeed against gunspeed. So he gave the killer a little encouragement. He realized it was working out when he finally caught the faint glitter of light on the killer's slow-rising gun. A percentage girl stifled a scream by ramming a fist in her mouth.

Ketchell continued fashioning his cigarette.

Any second now.

Then suddenly, treacherously, just as he was about to draw, the old enemy struck. Somewhere deep inside, some part of him was treacherously rebelling, reminding him of how often he'd played such a role as this in a bloody drama of bullets and death beneath swinging oil lamps or raging sun.

And once again the parade of the dead before his eyes. . . . Clint Feeley, Shawn O'Riordan, Tex Bitters, Long Tom Jones. Sometimes in the wind he would hear their graveyard voices . . . or stand alone in weed-choked graveyards feeling the dread hand of death upon his own young flesh.

'For God's sake watch out for yourself, young fella!' a shrill voice screeched, instantly jarring him out of his reverie. He was all speed and lethal intent

9

as he raked at his hip and flung himself sideways at the exact moment a shot rocked the room and something small and lethal whispered past his face so close he felt the bullet heat against his cheek.

As his gun came up he deliberately conjured up a vision of a town named Liberty, a blood-streaked bullwhip, a hated face, incredible pain – and a vow made in blood.

His blood.

Ramon Teel whipped out his six-tun with blistering speed as he dropped into a deadly crouch with his right hand whipping the black, filed-down, single action Smith & Wesson .38 clear of the leather. But Ketchell's blurring arm, hiss of breath and thundering shot were all of a piece, a lethal unity. Teel shuddered convulsively, staggered three uneven steps forward and crashed dead on his face.

The atmosphere in the saloon still remained tense and hushed when both sheriff and undertaker arrived together. Questions were answered, statements taken and the remains of a murderer toted off to the undertaker's before most everyone simultaneously felt the urgency of a strong double shot calling.

Ketchell lighted a fresh smoke, bought a bottle of John T. Smith and toted it across to a table by the wall where he sat looking both paled and relaxed now the deadly business was over.

And knew he'd silenced those nagging inner voices, at least for the time. . . .

Soon the normal buzz of conversation resumed, the blood was mopped up by the Mex swamper and a drunk tripped over a spittoon. Given just a few short weeks, folks would be hard put even to recall Ramon Teel's name.

After a time Ketchell was joined by the girl who'd called the warning. She was more than halfway pretty with fair hair and blue eyes, said she thought he was 'cute'. She told him she was from San Francisco originally, and he believed her. In the eyes of girls from old San Francisco you could always see the soundless sea fogs rolling in to their final shore. Her name was Cindy and he shared his John T. Smith with her for a time.

Cindy was pleasant company but John T. Smith was better.

He'd tasted hard liquor for the first time after killing his first man in Prescott, Arizona, nearly three years ago now.

The raw spirits had damn near choked him that day, yet warmed him all the way down and helped him forget what it felt like to watch the life rush from the eyes of a man you'd just shot.

Since then – a lot of John T. and a lot of dead faces. Sometimes the ghostly images refused to fade away, but whiskey always soothed his spirit. There was a girl from Tuscora in Mexico who used to rub his scarred back with it when it hurt. It rarely hurt any longer, just itched like crazy sometimes.

He absently rubbed his shoulders gently against the chair back and gazed off into those San Franciso mists and heard the foghorns of the boats calling to one another like lovers who had lost their way. . . .

'Have another, Cindy,' he said sharply, jolting

11

himself out of it. Then he remembered to smile and immediately looked ten years younger. He rarely smiled .

The girl poured herself another from his bottle, took a sip, turned serious. 'Ain't it risky, putting away all that red-eyed, honey?'

He slapped his flat belly. 'Iron insides,' he assured her.

'I don't mean what it will do to your belly, good-lookin'. I mean – don't they say you gunfighter boys gotta stay sober all the time in case someone sneaks up and shoots you in the back?'

He laughed, a short brutal, sound.

'Not me, Cindy baby, not old yours truly Floyd K.' He leant forward suddenly. 'Want to know why so? It's because I'm just too everlasting fast, is why. My hand is faster than the eye can follow. I was born fast and have gotten faster every year since I first—'

He stopped in mid sentence, eyes dropping to his glass. This was the sort of brag he'd used before he made his name. It had been necessary to pump himself up those days, but not now.

He raised his glass to his lips, sipped, grimaced. Even good old reliable John T. seemed suddenly to have lost its kick.

The girl watched him sympathetically. Although he was fully grown and strong with a hard, hand-some face, to her he still appeared too young to be a killer. It saddened her to think that likely before he even reached thirty he might meet someone faster and afterwards they would place him in the cold dark earth. Her Mexican boyfriend assured her that this was how all gunslingers ended their days.

'Floyd, honey?'

'Huh?'

'Where you heading from here?'

'South.'

'What's south?'

'Why, whatever you're looking for. Money, trouble . . . pretty women.'

'More killing?'

His eyes clouded. 'Look here, kid, if you are trying to point out the error of my ways then I can tell you I know what I'm doing and—'

She cut in on him, genuinely if momentarily actually concerned for this wild one. She didn't know he'd heard it all before. From pretty young women and from preachers who tried to redeem him. Old widows or young admirers – all felt it their duty to warn young Floyd Ketchell that should he keep on the path he was following he would wind up on a wooden slab in a cheap undertaker's in some flea-bitten no place town exactly like this one.

'Hey, honey, you listening to me? Suddenly you got a far-away look in them purty green eyes.'

She was smart, he realized. For in that moment he'd undergone yet another rapid change, was suddenly imbued with a sensation of welling excitement. The regret and the sour taste in the mouth following the gunplay were banished in an instant and he felt like a different man striding a brand new world.

His eyes swept the room and studied the faces – the unremarkable faces of the denizens of a low-life

Mexican dive in a nothing town a hundred miles from the region where he'd made his name. Yet even here they knew who he was, what he did. They'd read and heard about Ketchell – or Fast Floyd K. as some newspapers liked to tag him. Nobody could accuse him of being a nobody and a loser any longer . . . not like that sick and sorry young jasper they'd carried out of Liberty, New Mexico, three years back.

And he realized in that single visionary point in time that what had transpired here tonight against one of the most dangerous gunmen in the business, was sending him a message he'd been waiting for during three dangerous years behind the gun.

He was finally ready to travel back to revenge!

He rose in one fluent motion, straightening his shoulders. The girl made to rise but he placed a hand upon her shoulder and made her sit again. He flicked a ten-dollar bill from his shirt pocket and tucked it into her cleavage.

'Sorry, honey,' he said, 'but I've got miles to ride tonight.'

'But why? Surely you could just—'

'I just realized you're right, what you said about drifting around waiting to be killed. That made me think and suddenly realize I'm ready. Tee-totally goddamn ready . . . and it's the finest feeling I've ever had in my life!'

'Ready? Ready for what?' Her expression was concerned. He suddenly seemed wild and strange.

He made to reply but instead spun on his heel and strode for the batwings – a man with suddenly not one vital second to spare. Sure, she was sweet, and all she wanted was what was best for him, he realized. But only he knew what was best for Floyd K, just as he'd always known he would recognize the hour and the moment when one final test of his killing skills would raise him into the exalted company of the genuine princes of the gun.

He'd just faced one of the best in the business here tonight and killed him without even getting a graze. He was *ready*.

He was already on his way for the doors, brimful of energy and deliberately fanning the flames of the hatred that had driven him for three long years.

Halfway across the room, he heard her call. He stopped and glanced back to see her gazing after him with tears in her eyes. That jolted when it made him realize that he had actually come to mean something special to somebody. Even a skinny little much-handled saloon girl had her feelings and some kind of a heart – which put her leagues in front of himself. . . .

A gambler in a frock coat was too astonished to protest when Ketchell plucked the flower from his buttonhole, and retracing his steps, handed it to the girl and kissed her brow.

'*Adios muy caro*,' he said gently and was gone.

The girl held the flower to her breast and crossed to the batwings. In the velvet Mexican night outside, hoofbeats were already receding and her handsome lethal caballero was gone with the wind, leaving her with just a kiss and a flower for her breast.

'*Muy caro*,' she whispered to the stars, and felt the

15

beating of her heart beneath the flower. She remained on the shadowed gallery until her young man joined her, protesting he must surely drop dead at her feet if he didn't get a double tequila inside him within the next five seconds. And what the hell was she doing standing out here in the dark half-dressed and clutching a dumb flower, anyway?

She came back to earth and let herself be led back inside. She and Quint drank too much as they did most every night, and all too soon the handsome young gunfighter was washed from her mind.

CHAPTER 2

RETURN OF THE GUNFIGHTER

He remembered that lone chaparral. He was jolted back five years through the fogs of time to remember the blood, the fear . . . and the first cut of the bullwhip across his naked back which cracked away down over the hushed crowd like a rifle shot. . . .

'*Stop it*!'

Ethan Amador swung his great head at the sound of his daughter's frantic cry. Tara was struggling to break away from her brothers upon the porch of the Frontier Fast Freight office beyond the gaping mob. Coiling the blacksnake whip in huge hands, Amador signalled curtly for them to hold the girl fast. He then turned and swung the whip again.

Crack!

Now there were two livid welts across the boy's

17

muscular back, the first beginning to ooze crimson.

Hands thonged behind him and held down in a kneeling position in the dust by a pair of brawny Slash K riders, Floyd Ketchell emitted no cry of pain even though his young face was ashen with shock and sweat burst from every pore in the early morning chill.

Yet even despite the fact that the victim was barely eighteen years of age, or that big Ethan Amador was a renowned master of the blacksnake whip, none of the watchers here that grim morning honestly expected to be given the satisfaction of hearing Floyd Ketchell yell.

Somehow it just wasn't possible to imagine this one either giving away to pain or begging for mercy. Ever. Instead he had fought like a dozen hellcats as they'd dragged him into Front Street and had cursed Amador with a rare venom and fluency that impressed the many in the mob who had every just cause to hate the cattle baron.

Yet now, when there was nothing to do but take it, the boy took it in total silence.

The fourth stroke snapped and died. Amador had promised twenty. The cattleman never failed to live up to his word.

'I took you in, whelp!' the cattleman panted, swinging twelve feet of plaited leather again. He was panting some from the exertion already, for he was a huge man carrying too much weight and fuelled by bad temper. 'Took you in . . . treated you like one of my own . . . and in return you betrayed me!'

Five.

'Daring to put your dirty paws on my daughter—'

Six.

'—Figgered to marry her just so's you could get your greedy paws on a slice of Slash K!'

Seven.

Ketchell's back was torn and bleeding now, the vicious red cuts crisscrossing his flesh. His lips skinned back from locked teeth as he fought back the screams welling up inside. Mostly his eyes were shut tight, but when he opened them it was to see the whole town staring and gaping, all of them witnesses to his pain and humiliation.

Eight.

'He's already bleeding bad,' grumbled Sim Hogg, standing before his livery sucking on his pipe. 'Goddamnit, twenty could kill that boy!

'He'll get the twenty if it kills him or if it don't,' murmured deadbeat Sundown Trent at his elbow. 'I ain't never seen Big Ethan so mad afore – and the Lord knows he's been mad often enough.'

Heads nodded in mute agreement. True enough. Ethan Amador was renowned for being rich, violent and probably the most dangerous man in Box Butte County. A massive man with an iron will, he'd come to the county with the backside out of his Levis and four red-headed kids to raise back in the early days to grab wealth, power and prestige, grinding many a good man under his heel in the process.

Fifty thousand acres, ten thousand head of primes, his own bank and freight business, he could command twenty loyal guns and was answerable to no man.

It did not pay to stand up to cattle king Amador. Liberty already knew this and now young Floyd Ketchell was in the process of learning that vital fact of life.

Sheriff Al Yearly had learned this lesson a long time ago. Which was why the peace officer stood half-in and half-out his door watching the public whipping instead of attempting to stop it.

Yearly was a good enough man, but fond both of his job and staying alive.

Nonetheless, the lawman had still ridden out to the Slash K the previous night upon hearing that Amador intended punishing his star wrangler at dawn in Front Street.

It had been a courageous thing to do, considering the circumstances. But Yearly might well have saved himself the trouble. For it seemed Ethan Amador had finally woken up to what most folks had known for a time – namely that his daughter and young Ketchell were sweet on each other. Until then, Ketchell had seemed one of the very few men the cattle king seemed actually to respect and even like, and his rage was further compounded by what he saw as the treachery of the young horse wrangler.

There was no way he would tolerate any thirty-a-month cowboy besmirching his precious virgin daughter. He would make damned certain both Box Butte County and Ketchell remembered that for all time.

At the fourteenth stroke Ketchell's head fell in the dust and Amador signalled to the Slash K waddies holding the ropes to stretch him out.

Even the ghoulish who'd risen early to watch the 'entertainment' were beginning to feel queasy by this, and up by the Glass Slipper a man shouted, 'That boy's had enough, Ethan!'

It was like the cattle baron didn't hear. The whip rose and fell again and soon onlookers were beginning to turn away.

Upon the crowded porch of the Frontier Fast Freight, Tara Amador struggled to break free, but her brothers held her fast. They had their orders. Big, red-headed and slab-featured, Rod and Earl were very obviously Ethan's progeny, while the single resemblance between father and daughter was their fiery red hair. The girl was quite beautiful, even with tears running down her seventeen-years-old cheeks. Suddenly she got one arm free and instantly kicked her older brother in the shins. Rod quickly overpowered her but could not stifle her screams.

'Hush up, goddamnit, Sis,' Rod panted. 'You know he ain't going to quit.'

She did not hush. 'By God, if I were a man you would never hold me. If I were a man I would shoot your yellow guts out, and his too.' She spat in her father's direction and swung upon her kid brother.

'Johnny, don't just stand there like a goddamn boob. Do something. Floyd is your friend too.'

Young Johnny Amador looked sympathetic, sick and ready to faint away. Like his sister, he had their mother's looks, and was the only one of the four siblings with a gentle, artistic temperament. The youth hated what they were doing to Floyd Ketchell yet was powerless to do anything but stand and watch.

The girl filled her lungs.

'Pa – you bloody-handed animal. Leave him be!'

All Liberty was familiar with Tara Amador's fiery temper and flair for invective. Even so, that blast was savage enough to draw the attention of every pair of eyes upon the streets. Even Amador himself, whom many believed was cast from solid iron, swung his bull head to glare in her direction, jaw hanging open, the first red rays of morning etching granite features.

But then he swung back to Ketchell again, rage blackening his face now. 'So you've turned my own flesh and blood against me as well, curse you!'

Spent by her outburst, Tara slumped in the arms of her brothers and wept, bent over from the waist, her sobs weak and pitiful in contrast with the unrelenting slash of that whip.

Twenty.

Amador looped the blacksnake over his shoulder, his eyes glazed with – what? Satisfaction? Rage? Regret? He turned to stare dumbly at his ramrod and O'Fallion saw the madness there. The whip stirred in his hand and tall O'Fallion forced himself to step forward from the ranks of the Amador cowboys.

'That's enough, boss.'

The rancher froze with the whip still lifted, his stare fixed and mad. His ramrod spoke once again, forcefully this time. Slowly, seemingly by inches, the powerful arm came down until the bloodied lash lay in the deep dust. The rancher stared bleakly at the unmoving figure at his feet. Shaking his head like a weary beast he then turned on his heel and, coiling his whip as he went, trudged off towards the Slash K buckboard standing before the Glass Slipper.

'Get those ties off!' O'Fallion snapped. The ramrod winced when he looked at Ketchell's back. He quickly set to work, ordering the hands to tote the man across to the horse trough where he set about washing his torn and bloodied flesh.

Liberty looked on, horrified and mesmerized.

Doc Penrose supervised. When the wounds were cleansed to his satisfaction he applied some liniment. Citizens and Amadors continued to look on alike in total silence. O'Fallion took a flask of whiskey from his hip pocket and held it to Ketchell's lips, but the unconscious young man was unaware.

'Could be he might well need something more than liquor,' the medic said grimly. 'Something stronger, like prayers, maybe?'

The encircling cowhands stared at Penrose then back to Ketchell. Although young Ketchell was regarded as a mite flashy and over-feisty, there was scarcely a man on the Slash K who didn't like him. And now they were fearing the very worst.

Then the miracle!

A trickle of bourbon finally seeped through his lips and instantly Floyd Ketchell coughed and opened his eyes. For a full minute he stared blankly at nothing before turning his ashen face slowly to the medico. His lips moved but only Penrose heard his whisper. The man looked shocked, and a cowboy nudged him.

'What'd he say, Doc?'

'He . . . he wanted to know where his gun was.'

His words carried. Some appeared shocked, but just as many seemed impressed and even admiring.

'I told you that boy had guts to spare—' a cowboy began, but was cut off by O'Fallion.

'He doesn't want any gun,' he said sharply. 'Come on, help get him to his feet.'

They tried to assist but the victim only cursed them for their kindness, forcing them to draw back. Painfully, Ketchell raised his head and sighted Amador seated massively in his four-horse carriage, staring bleakly across at him.

Ketchell rolled saliva round his mouth and spat in the rancher's direction.

Cowboys and towners traded wondering glances. Minutes earlier they'd feared this man might die. Now he was delivering spitballs. What was he made of?

Ketchell pressed the flat of his hands against the ground and tried to propel his body forwards. He failed. Next he attempted to prop himself up into a kneeling position, but that too proved beyond him. His laboured breathing could be heard clear across the street. Ethan Amador swatted at a fly and looked on impassively, not even turning his head when his daughter let fly in his direction with a blast of truly excoriating invective.

For several minutes the bloodied figure lay motionless on its side, propped up by one elbow, with none daring to approach. Eventually he summoned up his strength and made yet another attempt, this time concentrating with ferocious intensity first to assume a kneeling position, then a short time later, he drove himself to stand upright.

Somebody cheered, a couple began to clap. The sounds died away when the rancher in the big rig swept the mob with his chilling glare of warning.

It was agonizing, watching Ketchell standing swaying there, not sure if he would walk or fall flat on his face. He did neither. When he finally felt stronger, he grunted at O'Fallion who came forward with his flask, his back to the ranch crew. The ramrod tipped the spirits to his lips and Ketchell gulped, coughed, swallowed again.

After another minute the tattered figure nodded faintly to O'Fallion, then turned stiffly to face the hotel where his horse stood tethered.

He started towards it.

It was agony to watch – the unsteady steps, the fixed and staring gaze, the fierce compression of the lips that held back the screams of pain attempting to burst loose.

At times his chin sunk to his chest, yet he kept pushing forward, at times merely gaining an inch at a step, yet never actually halting, nor looking at anything but that horse.

It seemed to take forever for him to reach his objective – his black shirt hanging from the pommel. Attempting to support himself, he rested a hand on the animal's neck, but it slid off and he fell to the ground beneath the horse's belly.

Nobody moved. Even sprawled there on his back in the dust, there was something about the bloodied figure that carried a warning. Keep your distance!

Ketchell blinked and stared upwards to focus upon a stirrup. Townsfolk held their breath as, time after time, he clutched for it without success. He was forced to lie motionless for several minutes more before mustering his resources again. At his next attempt, he was able to reach up an extra inch, grabbed steel and immediately hauled his body up off the earth until he was standing unsteadily at the horse's side.

O'Fallion did not move until his sixth attempt to mount up ended in failure. Ketchell said nothing as the tall ramrod cupped both hands and held them low until he was able to raise a foot to the support. The ramrod gave him a powerful boost and he settled into his saddle. With a grunt to O'Fallion, he took up the lines and used his heels to move the horse across open space to halt ten yards from the ranch buckboard.

The eyes of cattle king and cowboy met and locked. No words. Not yet. Ethan Amador was as impressive and intimidating in his massive arrogance as anyone had ever seen him as he met the other's deadly stare. And yet, there was something else in the cattle king's baleful glare, maybe a hint of doubt and uncertainty. For he had actually killed men with that great whip of his in the past, and none had ever sustained twenty full strokes before.

From day one he had always sensed the steel in this young waddy's make-up, but today's amazing defiance seemed to warn that there were others in the world who just might be as strong as himself. It also whispered that he was an old man who, for all his strength and power, had just failed to break a young one.

Ketchell's face showed only hatred – nothing else. The emotion shaped his every feature, hollowing his cheeks, lighted deep fires in green eyes. It seemed incredible that so much passion could be carried in simply a stare, the sheer force of which struck Amador almost like a physical blow.

'You should have killed me!' Ketchell's voice was a croak, but it carried. 'For one day I will surely kill you!'

He turned the mustang with his knees and rode away.

Almost as though seized by a sudden need to defend himself, Amador dropped his right hand to Colt handle. Instantly the sheriff raised a warning hand. The eyes of the two men locked and held. But in the end it was the cattleman who let go of his gun, looked around broodingly at the mob, challenging any man to speak.

None did.

For there was a full score of armed cowboys, all committed to protect the big cattleman and follow his every order. The crowd was fearful and it showed.

Amador sneered. He bossed a massive cattle empire, had a whole county in his hip pocket, and congressmen called him sir. He should worry about the threat of one half-grown saddle bum who would likely die before reaching the next town!

'Show your face in Liberty again and I'll hang you, boy!' he shouted from the buckboard. 'Hang you high, do you hear?'

Ketchell did not hear. He heard nothing, saw nothing. It was willpower alone that enabled him to ride a mile clear of the town limits before he crashed to ground and blacked out.

An hour later he was picked up by an alfalfa rancher from Kettle Drum. The man and his wife nursed him until the wounds on his back began to heal and close over. The couple knew who he was and what had befallen him, yet never spoke of it afterwards. Neither did Floyd Ketchell. At the end of the week he thanked them, tossed his last fifty dollars on their kitchen table and swung a leg over his ugly mustang.

And rode clear out of Texas.

He remembered that great pine tree.

On the worst day of his life he'd awakened from a delirium of incredible pain to see it looming above him like some other world monster with its massive arms outstretched wide.

Sheer desperation had seen him somehow crawl forward into the pine's shade and collapse, which was where the rancher couple from Kettle Drum had come across him.

The tree was now even larger that it had been five years earlier, almost to the day, but was patently recognizable as the same tree that had protected him from a potentially murdering sun.

Seizing a handful of pine needles he crushed them in bronzed hands and pressed them tightly against his face. He inhaled deeply, vividly remembering their pungent scent.

In that timeless moment it all seemed like just yesterday; the sun, the tree, the total agony in his back and the fire of his humiliation. The hatred rose in him more strongly and he encouraged it now, fanning it with the heat of memory that sent a shuddering jolt of anticipation through his entire body. Sheer emotion seemed to compress five whole years into this searing moment with such dramatic power that for a long moment he was forced to clench his eyes shut ... before finally managing to break the trance and will himself back to the normal zone of the here and now again.

He opened his eyes and said softly, 'Take me to town, old-timer.'

The ugly horse arched its neck with a sudden toss, reflecting a tarnished yellow sun in the moist jewels of its eyes. It sensed his excitement and responded to it by breaking into a quick, mile-eating lope that carried them towards the town of Liberty.

The place had changed plenty!

That was his first reaction as he reined in at the northern mouth of the main street. Prospered too, by the looks. Liberty had merely comprised Front Street bisected by three other cross streets, back then. It now comprised a dozen large blocks with solid brick and timber buildings rising all along Front. He glimpsed a new stage depot, assay offices, lawyers' chambers, any number of new saloons.

Cattle was king in the county and Box Butte County was virtually all cattle land. Amador would have to be a millionaire by this, he calculated, as he clop-hoofed in deep dust past the impressive Amador Banking Company. He would make a rich corpse.

Liberty didn't recognize him. At first.

There was little to link this bronzed stranger with the bloodied youth who'd somehow managed to defy death here five years earlier.

The town had boomed from beef and mining, yet had enjoyed anything but a peaceful life during that time. There'd been big money made, yet at high cost. The place might look peaceful and prosperous to the stranger, but the County Death Register at the law office would show otherwise. They boasted a sheriff and three deputies here, yet Front Street was never a stranger to the crash of guns or to the fast gun breed.

Yet this newcomer proved eye-catching enough to shake up the normal drowsy tenor of a sultry afternoon, and from bar windows, office blocks and all along the walks, folks paused in whatever they were doing to take a second look.

They saw a young man with cold green eyes who rode lightly with the suggestion of a coiled spring in his body. He sported a worn yellow hat, and a richly worked Mexican gunbelt and Colt were buckled round a slender waist.

The green eyes stared bleakly out from a lean face burned saddle brown by too many border suns.

The overall impression he created was that maybe he should come complete with a red tag fixed to his warbag to indicate danger.

'What's this the wind's blown in now?' an old-timer griped as the horseman passed by with a soft creak of leather and wisp of tobacco smoke. 'Cuss it, seems to me they're breeding them up even younger and meaner-looking every day.'

Heads nodded in agreement. Yet amongst the bunch loafing on the porch of the dry goods store, liveryman Sim Hogg stroked his bull jaw thoughtfully and squinted after the stranger's receding form. Hogg was renowned for two things in this town; criminal overcharging and a remarkable memory. The way the man suddenly rose out of his cane chair and pushed his hat back told them something had obviously piqued both his curiosity and suspicion.

'Nah, I don't think so. . . .' he muttered aloud. 'For a moment I thought—' He broke off and snapped his fingers. 'Hey, didja see that? The way he fingered back that yeller hat. By God and by glory – it is him after all!'

'Who?' growled a broken down old cowboy. 'Wild Bill Hickok?'

'You danged old fool!' Hogg retorted sharply. 'You used know him as well as I did when he rode for the old Slash K. Afore they nigh cut it in half, that is. That there is young Floyd Ketchell – so guess it looks like Amador's whipping never killed him like we all figgered it would have to do.'

To a man they appeared shocked.

31

Floyd Ketchell had never ceased to be a subject of idle talk and speculation among the sit-and-spit club here in the porch shade. They recollected there had been nothing heard of Ketchell for a full year following his leaving town more dead than alive. Then, one by one the stories had begun to come in – stories of gunfights featuring a man named Ketchell, said to be both fast and deadly.

The tales drifted in from Arizona, New Mexico, Kansas and as far off as Nevada. Most locals refused to connect the man Ethan Amador had whipped that day with this new name in the gunsmoke trade, until Chance Fowler of the Frontier Fast Freight here had actually seen him gun down a man in a saloon in Wichita eighteen months earlier.

After that, loafers with nothing better to do had followed his activities avidly in the press, some boastfully claiming him as 'Liberty's own'. And now he was back!

A buzz of excited speculation swept along Front like a brush fire in August and eventually overtook the cause of it before he reached the central block. Oblivious to the stir he was creating, Ketchell turned his mount in at the Glass Slipper Saloon, where a panting Sim Hogg finally caught up with him.

'Well, well!' the man shouted. 'Let me be the first to welcome young Floyd Ketchell back to home!'

The rider ignored him .

Ketchell's total attention at that moment was focused upon three horses all wearing the Slash K E brand, standing at the hitchrail swishing flies. He was puzzled by the addition of the letter 'E' to the old familiar brand. He finally swung a cold eye upon the man following him as he stepped down and twisted the reins round the tie rack, then hitched at his gunrig. Hogg slowly lowered his hand, his welcoming smile beginning to congeal.

'Floyd—'

'What did you ever do for me, Hogg?'

The man paled. Retracting his hand, he backed up a step, then turned indignant.

'Well, I don't see any need to welcome a man like that, young Ketchell.' He sniffed. 'Looks to me you must have started believing those things they say about you in the papers – about being the new gun king and suchlike.'

Ketchell held his flat stare a moment longer. He'd once come upon a copy of the Liberty newspaper containing an article covering that day he'd been whipped. Hogg, the writer, had appeared to half-agree that his punishment had been warranted.

Brushing past the man he deliberately made contact with one shoulder, sending him staggering. To Hogg it felt like a butt from a steer. He almost collapsed as Ketchell climbed the two steps and shoved his two-handed way through the batwing doors.

A large man was just coming out. Ketchell halted and stared at him, making no attempt to give ground. The fellow studied him a moment, then swore and stepped uncertainly to one side, chilled by that cold green stare.

The gunfighter nodded curtly and walked to the

bar, while Hogg darted in behind him, eager to be the first to spread the big news.

'John T. Smith,' Ketchell said, slapping the bartop.

His eyes shifted from the well-known face of Turk Henry to take in the varnished wooden walls and familiar tables. He switched to the faces, most of which were new, yet dotted with some that were remembered from the old days.

Three cowhands sat together at a faro layout, staring across at him. He recognized Coley Steubens who had worked with him on Slash K. The man looked back, curious but uncertain.

He heard the shot glass clunk on the bar behind.

'Say, young feller,' said the barman, 'ain't you young—'

'Yeah!' he snapped, not glancing at the man as he spun a coin on the bartop. He moved off in order to get his back against a wall before taking his first sip. Force of habit, and just one of the tricks in the survival game.

Emotion worked in him as the warm whiskey slipped down his throat. Rage and hate dominant, with just a flicker of nostalgia. But his thinking had never been clearer.

He was here to kill Ethan Amador and as many others who might want to die with him.

Nothing complicated about that, even though he didn't expect it to prove easy. Amador was more than ever king in this county and, as ever, protected by his sons, ranch hands, friends, the law – nothing like easy! On Ketchell's credit side, he was now armoured by a chain-lightning right hand supported by an iron nerve which had taken five solid years to develop.

He knew he could succeed at what he'd come to do, no matter what the odds. Today he was Nemesis with lightning in his right arm. He crooked a finger at Steubens.

The grizzled and bronc-stomped cowboy glanced uncertainly at his companions around the layout, then got to his feet and crossed to him. He smiled uncertainly, revealing a jawful of store teeth.

'Young Floyd!'

'Figured you'd remember me, Coley. Know why? On account you were one of them holding the ropes that day, cowboy.'

The man's weatherbeaten face turned grey. He realized this lean and hard-bodied man in the Mexican shirt sporting a tied-down .38 was surely not the same laughing young horse wrangler Tara Amador had fallen for once. This was a lethal-looking stranger he didn't seem to know any longer.

'I – I had to do what I was told, Floyd—'

'Don't tell me your troubles, Coley. Fact is, I picked you out to run a little errand for me.'

'Like what, Floyd?' The man was eager to oblige. Anything.

'I want you to ride out to Slash K and tell Amador I want to see him. Ask him if he can spare the time to drop by here in town, on account I'm five years overdue to blast his heart out his backbone.'

The cowboy wilted like he might faint. Ketchell didn't notice. In this long-overdue moment in time, he was riding a blinding, blue lightning-bolt of total rage and was conscious of nothing else except for the realization that at last this really was almost the end of a five-year trail at the close of which there would be Amador's death, and maybe even his own.

He snapped his fingers and gestured towards the batwings. Yet Steubens hesitated.

'You – you ain't just making a joke, Floyd?' he stammered, holding a sick grin.

'Do I look like I'm joking?'

'You mean – you mean you don't know?'

'Know what? Come on, either tell me what's eating you or get going—'

'He's finished.'

'What?'

'Amador. He got thrown off of a hoss two years ago and has been riding around in a big old wheelchair out at Slash K East cussing about it and giving his family and everybody else hell for breakfast ever since.' The man paused uncertainly. 'Guess you ain't saying you'd harm an old cripple, are you Floyd?'

Somehow Ketchell knew he was hearing the truth. He could feel tiny beads of perspiration suddenly erupt on his brow. When the long silence dragged on, the man said, 'Does this mean you might . . . you might change your plans then, Floyd?'

'It means he's a dead man and you got the job of telling him so – that's what it freaking well means, mister!'

The cowboy was nodding and trembling when

Ketchell shoved him aside and strode from the saloon, the batwings flapping into silence behind him.

He knew he must appear shaken in that moment. But inside he was iron. This information changed nothing. Had he just learned Amador to be six months dead, he would go dig him out of his grave and give him six in the guts.

Nothing less would give him peace for the rest of his life.

CHAPTER 3

THE FAST BREED

Swirling memories faded and ghosted away into the silence leaving a lone horseman staring across the trail at a solitary pine tree raising needle-clad limbs like entreating arms to an empty sky.

He sat motionless in the saddle vividly recalling five years back, waking from a delirium of agony beneath a savage sun to see that pine looming above him like something from a nightmare.

Somehow he'd found the strength to crawl into its shade, and it was there that the rancher couple from Kettle Drum had stumbled across him.

The pine seemed twice its former size five years on, yet was still easily recognizable as the thing he would always believe had saved his life that day.

He patted the solid trunk and shook his head. He was coming out of it now and the shock of what he'd learned earlier was finally receding.

Crippled!

Somehow he'd never envisaged Amador even growing older, much less badly injured.

Why had he never considered such possibilities? The answer was both immediate and obvious. In his mind's eye, Ethan Amador had always been pictured exactly as he had been that day . . . all-powerful, unstoppable, seemingly impossible to kill. But why had he not heard of the accident?

He nodded.

He knew why.

He had never read a newspaper in those five years, had never once trod Texas dirt. That had all been part of the iron resolution he'd made upon realizing he would survive his whipping after all. He'd wanted neither to hear nor know one solitary thing about the Amadors until the day he would return with a gun in his fist to settle his blood debt.

For to have heard something new and inflaming of Ethan Amador over that long span of time might have enraged him and driven him to return to this place before he was fully ready. While to have heard anything at all of Tara would have surely been too painful.

For a moment the girl he'd once loved intruded on his thoughts. But only for a moment. For Tara belonged to the past. He reckoned it highly likely a girl with her looks and class would be married now; half the young blades of the county had been crazy about her even way back then. How he would feel about her were they to meet now, he couldn't even guess. Love was barely a memory now. The only genuine emotion he'd experienced throughout those five years of self-exile had been a rage as big as Texas.

He shook his head slowly and refocused his thinking. In his mind he had always believed Ethan Amador would remain indestructible, incapable of faltering during his headlong journey through life, certainly never falling ill. He had always pictured the man huge, arrogant and in rugged good health the day he met him face to face and shot him down like a mongrel dog.

He was recovering his balance fast by the time he mounted up to make his slow way back to town. En route, he reassured himself, 'Nothing has changed. It could have been much worse. Amador might well be dead. But he's alive and still as big as ever, so the oath I swore a thousand times can and will still be fulfilled.'

The savage old bastard will still die, and by my hand whether he be crippled or whole.

This moment of renewed resolution was followed by a sudden jolt of hard-edged reality. Crippled or whole, Amador would still prove as hard to kill as the President. The man was ruthless, clever, surrounded by both kin and gunmen sworn to protect him even at the cost of their own lives. He would be a fool not to accept that while Amador breathed he would remain a seemingly indestructible and hate-powered giant. To forget that for even one moment could well see the one sacred mission of his life end in failure.

Of this he was instinctively sure.

Still engrossed in his thoughts, he later didn't remember reaching the town or stabling his horse. At the saloon, his brooding self-absorption remained intact until he heard a voice, as though coming from a great distance say, 'Floyd.'

Slowly, like someone emerging from thick fog, he turned his head and jolted back into the present. A girl stood before his table, her worried face somehow familiar.

'Who are you?' His tone was cold as he straightened.

She smiled. 'Jenny Prentiss. Don't you remember?'

He frowned in concentration, still not fully free of his dark thoughts. Then suddenly memory clicked in; sixteen-year-old Jenny Prentiss at the Cattleman's Ball – way back. They'd danced too often together and Tara had gotten jealous.

'Er . . . hi,' he muttered. Then, 'What are you doing working in a place like this?' And immediately regretted his words.

'Pa went broke,' she replied simply. 'Can I join you?'

He hesitated because of his deep mood. But this was really a very pretty girl with a soft face and shining brown hair. As well, she acted pleased to see him again, which was proving anything but common here. So he indicated the empty chair opposite, thinking: 'She looks too good, not only for this dump but for any saloon any place.'

'Are you all right, Floyd?'

'Fine.'

41

She touched his hand on the table. 'I was worried. You looked so strange when you came in.'

He forced a smile as he reached for the makings. 'Old home week. It can take it out of a man.' He frowned. 'But relax, girl, I won't bite.'

'I'm sorry, I just—'

'I reckon I can guess,' he said, rolling shag cut in a cupped hand. 'You're nervous on account of what folks are likely saying about me already.' He forced a grin. 'But I'm no different than I always was. Just older.'

She appeared to relax some, linking her hands together and leaning back a little. Licking tobacco and paper into a neat cylinder, he studied the girl's face thoughtfully. Part of him wanted her to go, the other part reasoned that company might be just what he needed most right now. There was also a need for further local information in light of what he had discovered that day. He'd always liked Jenny, would prefer getting his facts from her than from some bartender or saloon bum.

He reached into his pants pocket and produced a two-dollar bill. 'Go fetch a flask of John T., Jenny. We've got some talking to do.'

They were still talking an hour later.

Much of what she related he let go over his head in order that he could concentrate solely upon the history of the Amador family as it had evolved during his absence.

He discovered that the original sprawling Slash K had been split up following a series of rustling incidents compounded by endlessly bitter inter-family fights. It was now Slash K East and Slash K West, the huge east sector occupied by Ethan Amador and his two older sons, Rod and Earl, while Tara and young Johnny Amador together had wound up with the vastly smaller and poorer Slash K West.

The moment he heard exactly how the original spread had been divided, Floyd knew that the younger siblings had been brutally shafted by the old man.

Slash K West had more rocks, less water, difficult access and a predictably dismal future compared with the K East, which boasted lush pastures with a wide river flowing through and the potential to support a dozen families.

'There was always family conflict as you likely remember,' the girl went on. 'Especially between Tara and her older brothers. Rod and Earl were never what you might call kindly, gracious or loving in any way—'

'What you're saying is that they were always just a pair of bastards?' he said with a humourless grin.

'Something like that. Anyway, the split came some time after their father was hurt in a fall from his horse. Tara nursed Ethan for a time but then Rod and Earl feared she might influence him her way too much. There were endless fights and eventually the old man decided the time had come to settle the situation. Naturally he chose to live with the older boys and hand them the lion's share, for all three of those outsizers are brothers under the skin anyway.'

'So I recall. . . .' Ketchell was also remembering

that it was the two older brothers who'd reported his romance with Tara, so touching off the old man's outrage and leading to his own subsequent whipping and banishment. He owed that prize pair of bastards plenty also.

His back began to itch. He was not surprised, considering the way the past was crowding in on him here. He rubbed himself against the chair and nodded for the girl to continue.

He learned that worsening troubles for the family had erupted following the split-up. Clashes between riders from K West and East were a regular occurrence these days, while it seemed the only time the whole family got together was to thrash out law suits at the courthouse.

She hinted that Tara had become something of a shrew and 'hard as old nails', as she put it. He paid little attention to that. It stood to reason a young woman would have to toughen up if she wanted to operate a cattle outfit and deal with rustlers, crooked beef agents and her family all at the same time, so he reasoned.

Then he asked the question that came hard. 'Has Tara . . . met anybody, Jenny?'

She knew what he meant.

'There is this good-looking security man and gunman she hired to help her cope with her troubles. His name is Jubal Ralls and he's made quite a reputation as her troubleshooter and bodyguard. Comes from over Crane Crossing way. I-I don't know if it's serious between them or not. It's real hard to talk to Tara these days. Seems she acts more

44

like a mean guy than a pretty girl.'

'She's grown hard, you say?'

'I'm afraid so.'

He just nodded. Jenny and Tara had never gotten along, as he recalled. So he didn't expect a glowing report on Tara from her. He realized he'd expected to bump into Tara before this. Not for any particular reason, he mused – apart from the fact that maybe he still loved her. . . .

He frowned.

A gunman driven by hate couldn't afford to think about things like that, he chided himself. He was here on a mission which had nothing to do with love or pretty women. He would achieve what he came for. That was all that signified for him . . . as he rubbed his back some more and swallowed a little more of that fine John T. Smith. . . .

When the girl returned to her chores he found his restless mood seemed to leave with her.

He knew he would see Tara eventually, but likely wasn't ready for it just yet. So, instead of doing other things, or even doing nothing at all, he set off on a long walk through the twilight to shake off the whiskey fumes and clarify his thoughts in light of new information.

The notion that he would now have to exact his revenge upon a cripple disturbed him not at all. When he was flogged to within an inch of his life he'd been but a skinny youth of eighteen while massive Ethan Amador was at his physical peak. Surrounded by his hardcase crew that evil day, with the whole town looking on and with a dozen of his men to hold him helpless, he had been beaten the way you wouldn't treat a dog.

It was ironical that Amador had been prepared to kill him for his involvement with his daughter, yet now Tara was apparently banished herself.

He shook his head and his eyes were cold. Forget the deep thinking and the irony, Ketchell. Just concentrate on the one thing. Amador had set up the rules for this game of life and death, and that was the way it would be played out to the end.

Amador still must die, anyway he might get to kill him.

Then the inner voice . . . but what if he should die first. . . ? And was only too well aware that could well be on the cards.

He knew he would be six kinds of fool not to realize the enemy would suspect his reason for returning to Liberty by this. And that being the case, and if Ethan Amador was still the brutal bastard he'd been all his rotten life, then he would surely not be just sitting back in his wheelchair waiting for him to come after him. No way! Right now, at this very moment, he would surely be thinking of killing him first!

He turned another corner and the first person he sighted was Tara!

For a long moment he stood motionless and unobserved as he watched her make her lithe, impatient way along the western plankwalk just as the saloonkeepers were lighting their lamps. She was alone and wore a fringed shirt and split riding skirt. Red hair glinted like burnished copper in the twilight and she slapped the top of her calf boot hard with a riding crop as she strode through the twilight like she was rangeland royalty, which in a very real way she surely was.

He stepped forward. 'Tara?'

She halted and swung to face him. For just a moment that beautiful face appeared soft and defenceless as she lifted a hand towards him. Then in an instant the look was gone. She crossed to him with an arrogant assurance which he did not remember. The brilliant blue Amador eyes were those of a stranger.

'So— I heard you were back!'

Was this the greeting he'd expected after five years?

He scowled and tapped his chest. 'Tara, this is me. Remember?'

She stepped back from him. He automatically reached for her. She brushed his hand aside. 'Don't you dare lay a hand on me!'

'What?'

'You heard.'

She stood wide-legged, slapping her palm with her leather riding crop. She had grown taller and filled out to stunning proportions, was now not simply pretty but breathtaking. She was more woman than Floyd Ketchell had ever seen. But she was not the Tara he had left behind the night her father had tried to murder him with a blacksnake whip.

Again he stepped forward. This time she raised the crop.

'Keep your distance!'

Hard lines cut Ketchell's taut cheeks. He hooked thumbs in shell-belt and hauled his shoulders back.

'All right, Tara. So you're mad on account you've likely figured I've come back to showdown with your old man. Well, I won't deny it. I promised I would – swore it on oath, in truth. But it stands to reason you'd have had to know I'd be back some day.'

'Did it take you five years to work up the courage?'

The words stung.

'I was never short of courage,' he replied, green eyes glittering diamond bright. 'But I'll allow I did have to work up the gunspeed and the guts I knew I would need for the job. Because I knew your *brave* old man might likely throw twenty or thirty gunpackers at me if I ever showed my face here again.'

'And you got to where you wanted to be, didn't you? Oh, yes, we've all heard about the deeds of the famous gunfighter Floyd Ketchell back here in provincial old Liberty.'

A small crowd had gathered by this, yet prudently kept its distance while still remaining within earshot. Ketchell lowered his tone.

'Let's talk someplace else, Tara—'

'Talk? Whatever I have to say to you would be precious little. Besides, I'm in town on business and don't have any time!'

'After five years, you don't have time even to talk with me?'

'No more than you had time to write me!'

The accusation hit home. 'Look, I was near dead. For three months I had to try sleeping sitting up in a chair and leaning forwards—'

'You still could have written!'

'What the hell would I have said? That I was going to build up until I was fit enough to come back here and shoot your father down like the bloody-handed son of a bitch he is?'

The onlookers rolled their eyes. This was exciting stuff. When the girl swung to glare at them, a fat woman called an insult. Instantly Ketchell took three menacing steps towards the bunch, his face cold and lethal. As one they jumped back and immediately broke up. When he swung back on Tara he caught her dabbing at her eyes. He immediately felt awkward, maybe even a touch unsure of himself.

He said, 'There's a coffee place just a few doors along the s—'

He broke off as she whirled and started off. He thought she was quitting on him, and was cursing under his breath when she turned suddenly and swung into the eatery.

He followed swiftly to join her as she was seating herself at a corner table. He signalled for coffee for two, then sat opposite. Up close, she was even lovelier than he'd ever remembered.

'You didn't even write!' she repeated, and he sensed just how much she'd been hurt. Guilt gripped his guts. Why? Because he realized that scarcely once in those five years had he seriously

49

thought of one living soul but Floyd Ketchell and what had befallen him.

'Let me explain, Tara—'

'You might have at least told me if you were dead or alive. The first time I realized you were still breathing was a year later when I read about your killing a man in Flagstaff, Arizona!'

He leaned back against the leather, suddenly appearing years older. The man in Flagstaff had been a woman-killer with a $500 bounty on his head. His third kill. He tried not to remember the numbers.

'All right,' he said quietly. 'I was wrong. But my admitting that isn't going to make it any easier for you to accept that I've come back to kill your father. I know that. But I will kill him, if he doesn't get me first.'

'Do you still love me?'

He was startled by the question. He stared into blue-gray eyes which he remembered so vividly, and she returned his look gravely. He considered a long moment. Then, 'Yes.'

'Well, at least that's something.'

She was so matter-of-fact and almost flinty, even at that potentially tender moment, that he was forced to retort, 'I know I've changed, Tara. But you've changed so much I scarce know you.'

'Do you think I'm like a man?'

'Well, I . . . er. . . .'

'Oh, it's all right if you do. Because it's true. I learned to act and fight and think like a man to make sure I didn't finish up as an unpaid housemaid down on my knees all day cleaning up after hulking brothers whose attitudes to women are no further advanced than my father's. And he's Neanderthal. Yes, I stood up for myself and now I own my own land, I boss my younger brother about and I don't take any crap from anybody, not even the old man. If that makes me a man, then so be it.'

He began to grin. Didn't want to, just couldn't help it. From where he was sitting she seemed about as far removed from being a man, or mannish, as any female could ever be.

The coffee arrived but Tara Amador did not drink.

'So, I amuse you now, do I? You probably think that underneath this tough exterior I'm as soft and cuddly as every female you've ever slept with. Well, think again, gunfighter, or whatever you've become. I was in love with you once. You left me here at the mercy of four selfish men for five years to fend for myself and—'

'I never expected you'd miss me,' he said honestly. 'Your old man tried to kill me . . . the last conscious thing I said here was that I'd kill him . . . so you could hardly think well of me. But I still feel the same about you. It was Ethan I hated, not you. . . .'

He continued on in the same vein for a spell during which Tara Amador's face softened remarkably several times, until at one stage she appeared totally warm and feminine again. Yet by the time he finally ran out of words her expression was once again strong, cold and harder even than before.

'You never did lie well,' she said, tapping her crop upon the table top. 'And you haven't improved any over the years. You forgot all about me. That's the simple truth. But when it suited, you came back. Well, you are far too late, gunfighter. I never really needed you and I need you a damn sight less now. Take a tip from Tara and fork that apology for a horse you've got and ride out before someone shoots you in the back. And don't fret. I won't even notice you've gone.'

She rose and made to step past. Cat-quick, Ketchell jumped up and seized her by arm. The crop lifted, slashed at him wickedly. His right hand chopped her wrist, knocking the crop from her grasp. He seized her shoulders, ignoring the stares from around the room.

'You'll listen to me, damnit!' he gritted through clenched teeth. 'I thought of you a thousand lone-some times and then some, by God—'

His voice trailed off. She was no longer struggling in his grasp. He thought she appeared almost pleased at being manhandled, then realized she was looking, not at him, but at something behind him.

Before he could turn a quietly authoritative voice sounded from the doorway.

'Take your paws off of her, Ketchell!'

He spun, hand hovering over gun handle. A bunch of armed men stood shadowed beyond the double doorways. When none made a move, Ketchell slowly straightened before recognizing the man emerging from the line-up.

McCluskey was a brutish guntipper he'd crossed

trails with once down in Sonora. Low class scum, yet dangerous enough.

A second man stepped into the light and he realized he knew him also. But this one was no Rufe McCluskey.

Jubal Ralls had the reputation of a class gunpacker, and it was he who had spoken. He was a little taller than Ketchell, well-made and coldly handsome in a clean-cut way with dark eyes and the slim hands of a card sharp.

Their paths had crossed briefly at a remote way station in the heart of the bleak Gila Desert two years earlier. Ralls had been a top gun even then, Ketchell merely a comer. A shared drink, a few wary words, then the two went their separate ways.

Now they were meeting again in Liberty, Texas.

But what was a man of this calibre doing here? Suddenly several things he'd half-heard in local gossip began to fall into place.

He whirled sharply to put a quizzical stare upon Tara.

She smiled coldly.

'My employees and escorts, Mr Ketchell. Thank you, Jubal.'

He watched as Ralls entered the room like he owned it. The gunman moved directly to Tara's side and stood by her protectively. Ketchell glanced suspiciously from one to the other. Ralls was a handsome *hombre* with a rep as a lady-killer. There was something about the man's attitude that seemed somehow possessive and too sure.

'I was told you'd hired some backing,' he said to

the woman after a taut silence. 'They forgot to tell me what kind. . . .'

'Not that it is any of your business,' she replied tartly. 'I take it you don't care for my choice?'

'Not much, I guess. But I guess it's OK if you don't mind working with butchers.'

Tara stiffened and Ralls allowed his hand to drop to his hip.

Ketchell stood wide-legged, ready for anything and not prepared to retract. What he'd said was basically true, although he doubted Tara would believe it. Ralls was rated a top gun completely lacking in such attributes as a conscience or sense of honour. He'd even heard the man would as soon shoot somebody in the back as not, although he had no way of knowing if this were true. But the sight of a man of his calibre standing there with Tara in such a seemingly proprietary way was hard to take.

'I'd pick my words more careful, if I was you, Ketchell,' Ralls warned. 'It's four-to-one odds here in case you don't count so good.'

'I've stood off longer odds.'

'That's quite enough, Floyd,' Tara said sharply. 'I hired Jubal to help protect me and my place a month ago, and he and his men are doing a fine job. I can't order you to leave town but I will warn you not to interfere with me or my life.'

His stare held the woman for a long moment before he swung for the doors.

'She sure is a fiery one, ain't she, big-timer?' McCluskey sniggered as he went by. 'Told you where to git off, huh?'

Ketchell whirled faster than the eye could follow to smack the man under the ear with the flat of his hand, knocking him against a wall where he cracked his head hard before sliding dazed to the floor.

Ketchell paused to stare back at Tara and the gunfighter standing side by side. Neither spoke nor moved, and he was unsure if he'd won something or lost as he strode off to be engulfed by the night.

CHAPTER 4

DEATH STANDS CLOSE

Rubber-tyred wheels moved silently across rich carpet then clunked softly where the carpet gave way to polished cedar floorboards trimmed with metal edging that looked like gold.

Rod Amador moved swiftly to open the double doors which gave out onto the vast hardwood decking where his father sometimes liked to wheel himself vigorously up and down, often for hours on end. Other times he was just as capable of sitting massive and unmoving by the hour, brooding and unreachable. The endless wheeling sessions could abrade the nerves of family and staff, for somehow his massive silences could prove even more wearing on the nerves than his roaring rages.

Whenever the master of K East might 'withdraw'

into one of his silences, nobody could guarantee he would not finally emerge in a towering rage against some offence or slight, either real or imagined.

The wheelchair approached the waist-high safety railing where he hit the brake, wheels leaving a rubbery smudge a maid would erase later.

'All right,' he growled, a huge broad figure who somehow never seemed genuinely encumbered despite a useless pair of massive legs. 'Let's hear it.' He held up a hand as Rod approached. 'And don't editorialize, mister. Just give me the facts.'

Rod cleared his throat and glanced across at his brother leaning on the railing with a vast cattle range landscape forming a backdrop to his rugged figure. Earl shrugged broad shoulders and spread huge paw hands in a way that said clearly, 'Tell him whatever he wants to hear . . . you know he'll find out anyway.'

The brothers worked in synchronization most times. It was one way to survive in this place. Each was physically powerful and hard-driven by nature, was rightly feared both here and across the county. But at no stage, either singly or together, did they ever get to feel they were in control whenever the old man was about. Or certainly not as strong as they passionately wished to be.

'Well, Ketchell's been covering a lot of ground,' Rod reported, folding big arms across his chest. 'Drinks some, talks to a lot of people—'

'Including your sister,' the father broke in. He twisted in the chair. 'How come you didn't report that first thing, mister?'

'You didn't give me time to get round to it.'

'You were scared to tell me!'

Rod flushed and compressed his lips. He made no retort. They rarely did. But watching his brother closely, Earl sensed the day fast approaching when they would finally stand up and lash back. When both towering redheads would finally kick back and grab for the reins of power – and pray they survived. . . .

Earl nodded violently in support of that rebellious thought. Their long-awaited time must come, and soon . . . and surely there had been signs of late that their father was at long last beginning to fail? Maybe so. In the meantime, when the dictatorial old bastard said jump, you jumped.

'Well, get on with it,' Ethan growled. Then sat, hunched and massive in his chair staring out over the starlit rangeland while Rod furnished his latest report on Floyd Ketchell.

A highly unusual situation prevailed. Mostly when a problem arose on Slash K East, Ethan would issue orders instantly and the matter would be dealt with promptly and often with brutal efficiency. Yet for some reason routine had not been invoked or action orders yet delivered, regarding Floyd Ketchell. For his hulking sons, this puzzling and uncharacteristic attitude was beginning to arouse suspicions.

There could be no denying that Ketchell had made a powerful impact upon the entire county since seeming to rise out of a five-year-old grave. The smiling boy who'd once ridden for Slash K had returned a menacing presence with a personality that matched his reputation as gunfighter and even killer, which any man would be a fool to ignore.

The brothers had already confronted the man from the past on their father's orders. For reasons of their own, Rod and Earl downplayed the impression Ketchell had made in their report back to Ethan. In reality, that brief meeting had affected each man powerfully. They would eat ground glass before admitting it to anybody, but Tara's former sweetheart had almost intimidated them both, something nobody had ever managed to do. With the exception of the huge-shouldered presence studying them from the wheelchair, that was.

Silence. Then the father snapped, 'And the rest?'

'What?' Rod replied.

A hand smacked an armrest with a sound like a rifle shot.

'The reason he came back of course, you damned fool!'

'Er . . . nobody seems to know, but—'

'I'd damn well know if I clapped eyes on him for just ten sec—' Amador broke off abruptly, his expression suddenly altering. 'And by God and by Judas that's what I will do. If you want a job done in this life, do it yourself. Go ready the coach – no! Too conspicuous. I'll go in that girly little buggy you used to go courting in before that town whore handed you your marching orders. Well, don't just stand there. Get busy!'

Fifteen minutes later a light trap and pair

wheeled away from the headquarters with six heavily armed cowboys riding escort. The rig spun smoothly away down the gravel drive and clattered across the river bridge to quickly vanish along the town trail.

Rod groaned and stretched hugely, leaning against the rear wheel of the stationary trap standing in the half-light at the corner of East and Main. Eyes gritty with fatigue he tilted his big red head back to stare at the heavens, hoping to sight something, anything that he might focus on to help him stay alert.

There was nothing up there. No shimmering stars, no stray meteors or shooting stars streaking across the vast blackness. Only the eternal sameness, the dark arch of space dwarfing this small scatter of earth life standing beneath the limitless black cone of night.

He groaned in protest and made to complain. Before he could do so, a riding crop jabbed hard into his shoulder and his father's voice rumbled from the darkened interior.

'Stay alert, you damned loafer! By God and by glory, it must have been watered whiskey I was drinking the day you were conceived, you great—'

'Boss!' a voice called urgently from a darkened porch close by. 'Just coming around the corner. . . .'

Everyone froze. In an instant the only Slash K figure visible was the towering bulk of Rod Amador propped up against a fore-wheel, hat tilted over his face, pretending to be drunk and almost out of it as the footsteps approached.

The two men passing by beneath the street lamp glanced in the direction of man and rig but didn't slow, their voices soon murmuring away to silence.

'Pa!' Rod hissed urgently. 'That was him!'

It seemed a long time before his words drew response from the interior of the trap.

'I know who it was, moron. I see he's changed some, but not all that much. Once a nobody, always a nobody. All right, I've seen enough. Take me home. And if we hit that chuckhole by Bennett's farm gate again, some damned driver had better get used to scratching one-handed. Well! What are you waiting for? Move!'

Within moments the street lay deserted again. It was two-thirty in the morning. The K East party had waited over three hours and watched hundreds pass by before Ethan Amador had caught one thirty-second glimpse of the man who wished to kill him.

He did not speak once during the return ten-mile journey. His silence could mean everything or nothing.

Tobacco smoke trickled from Ketchell's lips as he watched sunrise break through misty cloud and fling hazy golden bars across the horse yard at the corner of Marcy and West Street South.

He didn't blink once throughout the silent minutes that followed which saw the first early-risers go tramping by on their way to stables, store or saloon to ready for the working day ahead.

Most saw him standing there, some pointing him out to one another. Nobody could figure what he

61

might be doing there in his flash yellow hat with that .38 thrusting aggressively upwards from a cutaway holster. But a couple of old hands reckoned they could guess educated. 'Looking for trouble is my bet, Sim.' And, 'Only hope it ain't trouble with us, pard.' And nudged one another nervously and glanced back over their shoulders as they passed from sight.

Ketchell was oblivious to everything but the old horse yard. The site was overgrown and plainly no longer in use now. There was nothing left to suggest that it had once been encircled by a throng of citizens watching a huge man administer the worst whipping this town had ever seen, and hopefully might never get to see again.

But in the eye of his memory he could see it all crystal clear, and his body again felt a ghostly sensation of that great pain which fanned his hatred white-hot and unforgiving.

While the fingers of his right hand stroked gunbutt and he didn't even realize it.

Yet by the time he had made it to the all-night chophouse he seemed totally relaxed and unaffected, suggesting he might be as skilled at acting and concealing emotion as he undoubtedly was at handling a bucking .38.

He entered the eatery and gazed round. Somebody had told him Tara Amador stopped by here for breakfast fairly regularly, but there was no sign of her today.

For a moment he seemed to reflect a hint of uncertainty, or was it puzzlement. Then an inner voice murmured, 'What the hell do you think you are doing? You disappear five years ago then suddenly ride two hundred miles to kill her father. So now you're looking to bump into her and maybe buy her some chow? You must be loco, Ketchell. Maybe you need a drink – a big drink. After that maybe you should go take another look at enemy territory, instead of day-dreaming here like a fool. . . .'

He grunted and strode swiftly away, deliberately flexing scar-thickened shoulders to invite back dark memories. Slowly but surely the rage returned, and soon Tara was forgotten.

Rod Amador concluded his lengthy report on the situation in the south, most of which focused on the Paradise Mine. The spread was vying with rival ranchers for the exclusive contract to supply meat for the diggers in the new iron ore mine down there in the boondocks which, if secured, could lead to the K East expanding to become the biggest beef suppliers in all Box Butte County.

Silence fell upon the uncovered teak deck for some minutes after the report was concluded.

Although accustomed to the old man's habits, both sons started when he suddenly brought his chair whipping around and propelled it violently forward.

'All right, tell them to get out the coach and be ready to leave in a quarter hour!' he barked. 'We're going to town!'

'What in hell for?'

For some reason he could not define, Rod was growing bolder and more outspoken these days, had been doing so instinctively ever since an unexpected element had entered their lives.

An element named Ketchell.

The oldest son was already halfway certain that the sudden return of his sister's former lover, complete with his gunslinger rep, might have achieved the impossible, namely had a negative effect on the old man.

This was hard to believe, he knew.

For Ethan's power had always been absolute. Yet every gut instinct told his giant offspring that a definite chink had appeared in the old bastard's armour. Something had changed him, and he was betting it was Ketchell. For deep down where he kept all his many secrets, Rod himself had experienced some kind of weakening in his bowels the first moment he'd clapped eyes upon Ketchell. That man – and he was very much a man now despite his youth – radiated danger; it was simple as that. But the suspicion that he might have affected the old man in the same negative way was stunning. Nothing intimidated Ethan Amador. Yet how else would Rod explain the undeniable fact that his father was no longer at his intimidating best, had not been ever since the moment Floyd Ketchell had strolled by their rig in town.

Rod had prayed for years for the day when the fierce old bastard faltered, which he sensed could be coming sooner rather than later. The suspicion that this day had come invested him with a new-found courage.

When he spoke his manner was scarcely confrontational, yet there was an edge to it that had never been there before.

'Well, damnit? Whyfor are we going to Liberty?'

'Because now I've got to size up this son of a bitch that's got you two walking on eggshells for myself,' came the deep-voiced reply. 'I'm deciding if he's worth killing or do I just shove money at him to get him out of our hair.'

He was forced to hit his brakes while Earl opened the sliding doors. Over his head, the brothers traded glances. He sounded serious, but you couldn't always tell.

As they entered the lavishly appointed room, Rod suddenly moved to block the chair's progress.

'What the hell—?' his father began, but was cut off.

'It's time we discussed this, old man. All of us. This son of a bitch looks dangerous. So we've got a right to know it if you're looking to tangle with Ketchell, and you know it.'

For a moment it seemed the man in the chair would begin ranting. Instead he bit his lower lip, shook his head and leaned back against the leather cushions, staring stonily at nothing.

'I'm no fool,' he rumbled. 'If I'd thought that bastard would be easy I'd have sicced you and the hands onto him soon as we sighted him last night. But I saw him and, thinking over what I saw – and felt, I'm prepared to try and talk sense rather than—'

'You want to *talk* to him?' Earl was astonished.

'And why not?'

'He hates your guts is why – goddamnit!' Earl gestured wildly. 'Judas Priest! Sometimes you're smart as they come but then there are times when you can sound almost dumb—'

He broke off sharply as a warning light leapt to the old man's eye. He made to apologize but was waved into silence by the sweep of a massive hand.

'If it wasn't for the pressure of the Paradise contract, and all these stinking section-ranchers hereabouts – including your own sister – banding together like a dog pack to bid against us and maybe steal a million-dollar contract from under our noses, I'd send you and the boys off into town right now to put that son of a bitch under the dirt.'

He suddenly fell silent. The two who knew him best studied him in puzzlement. The words were pure Ethan but somehow his manner did not quite match his verbal belligerence. Again that astonishing thought. Was it remotely possible the old bastard could really be uneasy about one lousy guntipper?

Their stares locked over the grey head. They were largely indifferent to Ketchell, mainly because they were not the ones who had once flogged the upstart to within an inch of his life. That was the old man's worry – and it really seemed to be worrying him. They only fretted about money. Money and power. When they dreamed nights they dreamed exclusively of their running the combined Slash Ks between them with the old man rotting in the grave, and Ketchell just a dim memory.

Rod was uncertain if he was reading his father right. Yet he felt confident enough now to attempt to swing this unexpected situation to their advantage, if they were smart enough.

He said reasonably, 'OK, the way I see it, Ketchell just might listen to reason – and a good deal. But not coming from you, pa. Stands to reason. But Earl and me know what's needed. If you want to get him out of your hair without a showdown, why not let us parley with the flash bastard and see what we can come up with.'

Ethan Amador detested anyone attempting to influence him, rarely tolerated it. He sensed that had this situation evolved a year or two earlier, he'd have had Ketchell in his grave by this. Not now. Deep down in his vicious psyche he privately realized he was far less the man he'd once been and now bitterly and resentfully might have to rely on others to protect him and save his life.

He brooded for a spell longer, then reached a decision in characteristic style.

'Do it. If you succeed in steering that butcher away from us, at least for the time being, you'll be rewarded. We can kill him later, if he's still around. Snuff him out like a bug. But right now that contract is what's most important. So get moving, and if you fail—'

He left the unfinished threat hanging in the air as he pumped his wheels and shot away in the direction of the study.

The brothers traded looks. Their expressions were often unreadable to others but usually each intuitively knew exactly what the other was thinking. They still didn't like this situation. At the outset they'd regarded Ketchell as an irritant, nothing more. Now it was different. The more they saw and heard of that gunner the more they saw him as a genuine danger.

But encouraging them was the fact that if things went wrong, K East had more than enough gun power to account for any threat no matter how large, much less just a single guntipper with a grudge.

They wanted to defuse the Ketchell situation in order to concentrate on the Paradise contract. That was important to them. For if they achieved that successfully they might feel emboldened to initiate their long-planned move to shoulder the failing old bastard aside at last and take over as they had yearned to do all their lives.

And if Ketchell was still around, they might even get to organize a double funeral.

Their thinking was ruthless and brutal. But, after all, they were their father's sons.

He was finding his new quarters at Mrs Doolin's rooming house on Dodge Street far more to his liking than the hotel had been.

His large and airy room was almost stylish with two cane-bottomed chairs that didn't sag beneath your weight, plus running water.

But what he liked best was the brass bed,

followed closely by the stained oak dresser and washstand that reminded him of that place he'd stayed at in Dodge City the year he'd gone buffalo hunting on the plains with a party of politicians from back East.

Ketchell grinned as he stood in the centre of the room wearing only Levis while he dried his back with a big black towel. He was whistling but wasn't sure why. For the harsh reality was that this was yet another day running by smoothly, and he still hadn't killed anyone, was yet to face the man he'd dreamed of killing every night over five long years.

He moved to check himself over in the good Mrs Doolin's mirror above the mantelpiece. It was flanked by a pair of crockery dogs which were terrorizing a crockery parrot with a broken beak.

'You're just using up time, Ketchell,' he accused his image in the glass. 'Getting into brawls, drinking whiskey, chasing after women who don't want to know you – one woman leastwise. And you're halfway smart enough to know that every hour you fritter away is another hour of life you're handing the bastard you came to kill. And who knows? If you dally long enough the old mongrel might move first and get to put you in the ground instead. . . .'

He shook his head, finished dressing, buckled on his gun and light-footed along Mrs Doolin's thick-piled stairway carpet. He emerged on the street just as the lamp lighter was setting off on his rounds.

Inhaling deeply he strode past the stage depot.

He failed to glimpse Yearly until the lawman suddenly emerged from a doorway ahead to block his way.

'What's the big hurry, Mr Ketchell?'

The lawman hadn't changed much.

'Who's in a hurry – Al?'

Yearly flushed. 'By Taos, time hasn't done much for your manners, I can see. But I'm not concerned with your character, mister, only your intentions. You see, I've been waiting to catch up with you to ask you something important, Ketchell. Namely, are you still a truthful man or maybe all that's gone down the drain with everything else you had once, but have plainly lost—'

'What are you trying to say?'

'I'm saying straight to your face that I don't intend to stand by and just twiddle my thumbs if you figure you can just ride back here after all this time and start dealing out your own six-gun kind of law—'

'Are you asking if I came back to kill Ethan Amador?' He didn't afford the sheriff time to respond. 'Sure you are. It's written all over you. Well, the answer is yes. What he did to me was a crime that he's never been called on to answer for . . . especially not by you. So, I'll kill him. If anybody tries to stop me I'll kill them too.' He started off. 'So I'll see you when the grapes get ripe, Yearly – you gutless fraud!'

The lawman was shaken as he watched him stride away. He'd half-expected Ketchell to lie about his intentions. He felt a cold sweat gathering on his brow as the lithe figure disappeared from sight, and wondered if maybe he had just made a blunder. For now he knew the gunfighter's intentions, shouldn't he feel morally obliged to do something about it?

Should . . . maybe. The question was – would he? Yearly was an honest man who made a good fist of law and order in a town prone to violence and dominated by the Law of the Strong.

But all he could think of was how bad things might get here should Ketchell actually go after the biggest man in Box Butte County. People could get hurt in a situation like that and it stood to reason that the town lawman would be at greater risk than most.

It was a bad time to think how much he didn't want to die.

The husky timber-cutter could really fight. His left hook beat a tattoo like a trip-hammer while his straight right jabs would flatten a man's nose fast if he didn't keep bobbing and weaving.

Ketchell kept bobbing and weaving.

He still wasn't sure how the fight began. He'd gone from the eatery to a dimly lighted working-men's saloon on Buck Street, was working on his second shot of whiskey when someone hit some-body else, and when another party altogether called him a name, he'd socked him in the jaw.

It was all Tara's fault.

At least so he told himself as he ducked and weaved, trying to set himself up for a knockout punch as his rugged adversary ducked and weaved around him like a professional prizefighter.

'Your hands, Ketchell!' he chided himself under his breath as he back-pedalled. 'You're supposed to take care of your hands. . . .'

Next thing he knew he was rolling amongst the cigar butts on the floor with the timber-cutter attempting to stomp on his head which was ringing like a gong from a left hook he hadn't even seen coming.

He was relieved to look up and see the badges coming in. The ruckus was all over in seconds and he sprang erect and was preparing to lie his way out of it when an irate Sheriff Yearly took hold of his adversary and promptly clapped the bracelets on him.

'Been looking for you ever since that fight over at the livery, McCluskey,' panted the law. 'As for you, Ketchell, if you want my advice you'll take your trouble-making ways somewhere else and forget to come back. Savvy?'

Back on the street, Ketchell felt he'd escaped lightly. He rubbed his jaw and leaned against an upright. It was Tara, he knew. She was clouding his mind and affecting his judgement. Meeting her again had been a huge jolt, while realizing just how far apart they had drifted over the years caused an ache that simply would not let him concentrate on the real reason he had come back.

He straightened up and strode on down the centre of the street, swinging his arms and breathing deeply. 'Remember why you're here, gunfighter,' he chided himself. 'And it's not to brawl in bars, and it sure ain't letting women make you forget why you came.'

He sleeved his mouth and squared his shoulders, drawing in lungfuls of cool, clean Texas air. By the time he reached the intersection he was feeling pretty much as he had done upon his arrival three days earlier. The hardness was back, the resolution. Hard, cold and resolute. 'From here on in, Ketchell – stay focused on just the one thing – then be ready to ride on out when it is all over and done.'

For revenge five years overdue was surely everything, and anything else just buffalo dust.

In retrospect he knew that brawl tonight had erupted simply because he'd drunk too much. And that he drank too much because he knew he was dodging the grim business that had brought him back in the first place. Revenge. He was back on track now.

Tomorrow he would ride out there and decide exactly how he would get to his enemy and put him in the ground. He'd not planned on letting him live even this long.

Because lawyers were still very much in short supply in that part of vast Texas, and due to the fact that he looked more like a lawyer than anyone else in the county, with his long, suspicious nose and polished pince-nez, folks just called him Lawyer Preen.

He was a fine attorney-at-law and a serious citizen to boot. He was smart, discreet, and considered himself a good judge of character. He saw most kinds across his desk in his compact little office above the Frontier Fast Freight, and believed he could often predict a client's business and intentions before he even opened his mouth.

Yet studying the hard, hawklike young face across his desk today he had to admit to a certain puzzlement. He was not part of the Liberty scene at the time of the historic incident between Ethan Amador and Floyd Ketchell, but naturally knew all about it. He believed he already knew Ethan Amador as well as he would ever wish to, but he had no clear insight into Floyd Ketchell.

For young bronzed men with ice-cold eyes and tied down revolvers rarely consulted attorneys-at-law. His visitor with the violent history behind him seemed almost boyish in some ways . . . if you were prepared to overlook those sub-zero green eyes.

But a client was a client, he reminded himself. Even if his client had walked right in without being invited and dropped his hat upon his desk before occupying the vacant chair opposite.

'Mr Ketchell, I believe. Is there something I may assist you with?'

'They claim you're straight, Preen?'

'Well, I suppose—'

'Honest men are hard to find these days.'

'Ah—'

'Especially here in Liberty. But I hear that if I want to get something straight in this town I should come see you. Never had any dealings with any attorney before and—'

'Mr Ketchell, is there something I can do for you, sir? Something specific, perhaps?'

Ketchell raised dark brows, impressed by the man's natural authority.

'Sure there is. I want you to tell me everything you can tell me about the Amador family.'

Preen swallowed. He'd heard of the violent events involving this man and the Amador clan, none of it pleasant. He managed a thin courtroom smile.

'What precisely is your interest?'

'You gotta know well enough!'

'I assume you are referring to the storm of gossip that's been revived concerning you and this family since your return?'

'Right.'

'Well, for your information, I am fully conversant with events involving you and that family some years ago. I have also been told that you have returned to Liberty with the express intention of murdering my former client, Mr Ethan Amador?'

'That I surely have.'

The attorney's jaw sagged. He had not expected such candour.

'But that's not what I came to see you about, Lawyer Preen,' Ketchell said. 'Tell me straight, what is happening out there on the two Slash K ranches right now? I hear stories of family feuds and wrangling over rangeland rights, cattle deals and suchlike. That's why I decided to come see somebody who might give me some straight answers about that whole set-up.'

Preen studied his visitor. He recalled how a drunken Ethan Amador had spoken of Ketchell in his hearing once – half in hatred yet partly in grudging respect. Whether Amador ever regretted the fearful punishment he had administered to Ketchell Preen didn't know. He considered it unlikely. He suspected that savage Indians from the Osage Hills might show more humanity than the Amador clan.

He settled back in his chair and told Ketchell what he could legitimately explain about the current personal and commercial situation existing between the Amador families on the two Slash Ks.

Ketchell was presented with a picture portrait of a family divided between father and two eldest sons on Slash K East, and a smaller and less successful operation on K West, now in the hands of Tara and Johnny.

Ketchell pressed for even greater detail, thinking he would not even be here in this stuffy little office, but for Tara.

He'd never anticipated just how powerfully meeting up with her again might affect him.

Yet he fought against this. He'd known from day one he could easily lose his life trying to kill Ethan Amador. Yet nothing could stop him trying. Gun him down, hightail into the mountains and never see Liberty again.

Quick, neat and final.

Only thing, he was now burdened by the suspicion that Tara could be living in some kind of peril, and that was distracting him from his purpose. Or leastwise, he'd come to believe that was the reason he had not struck by this.

Right now he needed convincing he could do

what he'd come to do without endangering Tara. He'd sought that reassurance from Preen. Yet by the time the man finished talking, he reckoned that might prove impossible.

Lawyer Preen obligingly furnished facts, figures, probabilities and opinions concerning the future of the family, until he could not absorb any more.

But the one question he could not ask, was what the attorney believed would happen to Tara should he blast her father into hell.

It was silent for a spell now. Preen had overcome his initial unease with the intense gunman. He knew he could kick Ketchell out then go see the sheriff. But what would that achieve? Talking was no crime. Besides, he was lawyer enough to want to change a grim situation rather than back away from it.

'That family revolves around the father – for all his many faults,' he said quietly.

Floyd acted like he didn't hear that. 'So, explain a little more about this beef contract with the iron-ore mine you mentioned earlier. Seems to me if that could be settled, then K West and K East might stop sniping at one another finally and might even settle down to getting along?'

'It was the discovery of big iron-ore deposits at Paradise thirty miles south several months ago that lit the fire between Slash Ranch East and West, Mr Ketchell. Paradise lies at the tail end of no place on the fringe of the desert and expects to become home to three hundred miners before it's done. All those hungry miners wolfing dawn beef three times a day means a fortune for some cattleman. In this case, both K spreads went after the contract and next thing we knew there were shootings, night raids, several fatalities and all but open warfare between those siblings. The law doesn't seem able to handle the situation . . . so that is how it now stands. . . .'

'Do you reckon the Amadors on K East would actually harm Tara and Johnny if this fight for the contract didn't go their way?'

A shrug. 'Who knows? I only believe Ethan is totally ruthless, and I regret to say that quality appears to have been passed on to his progeny.'

After a long minute's silence, Ketchell suddenly rose.

'Obliged,' he grunted, dark brows frowning. 'Send the account to the hotel.'

'Anything else, young man?'

'You say you've been speaking to Tara. Did she . . . did she mention me?'

'As a matter of fact she did.'

He looked up sharply. 'Such as?'

The attorney spread his hands as he came around the desk. 'Generalities, a few specifics.' He halted. 'She did say she considered what befell you five years ago was quite indefensible . . . which of course it was. She also remarked on how light-hearted and peaceable you were . . . back then. . . .'

'Before twenty cuts of a blacksnake whip, you mean?'

'Mr Ketchell—'

'Subject closed, attorney.'

'Then you still intend to—?'

Lawyer Preen's unfinished sentence hung in the air as the door closed sharply on his client's back. Turning back to his desk, he rested the heels of his hands upon its surface and sighed. He had wanted to believe that in telling Ketchell what he wanted to know he might have been able to steer him away from this terrible course he seemed set on.

He felt certain he had failed.

Times like this a man could not help but wish he might have chosen another profession.

Danger country.

In the deep of the Texas night, with the stars too dim to shed light across the sleeping earth, a shadow stirred within deeper shadows beneath massive trees upon the North Forty section of Slash K East. Then all was still again.

An after-midnight wind rustled through the stand of oaks rearing tall and stately on the southern flank of Homestead Hill, then died away before reaching as far as the group of handsome buildings standing upon the plateau.

The headquarters comprised a sprawling circular compound, enclosing barns, corrals, outbuildings and holding yards, in the middle of which stood the centrepiece ranchhouse, the Amadors' castle and fortress.

The unseen night-comer sighted the cluster of dimly lighted buildings the moment he emerged from the woods a half mile to the northwest.

He was aware of the danger yet his heartbeat remained just as steady as if he were relaxing back at the Golden Slipper in town with a large whiskey in his fist.

For Floyd Ketchell and danger were old trail partners, and should tonight prove riskier than anything he'd ever attempted before, then he was ready for it. He'd imagined this night and this hour every day of his life for the past five years, knew now that nothing less than total revenge would bring him peace.

All that remained to be decided was exactly how, when and by what means that vengeance would be taken.

He was there a long spell. Crouched in back of a hillside boulder a mile above the sprawling headquarters, he let his mind travel beyond his moment of final triumph to the future.

It would be stark and simple: old man Amador in his grave and Floyd Ketchell drifting across Texas, triumphant and free as a jaybird.

That image of some distant day in the future had been his driving force for too long. He felt realization was close at hand, already far beyond the reach of any power or force to stop it.

He grunted and moved on across the shadowed hillside. He was travelling light. No shell-belt or hat. Just a tiny but lethal .22 pistol in his pocket and a Bowie in his belt at the back. He wore light shoes and nothing that might glint or rattle. It took ten intensely wary minutes to reach the first of the outlying outbuildings, where he hunkered down at a corner then instantly threw himself flat and motionless at the sound of footsteps.

Slow seconds ticked by before the dim figure of a nighthawk afoot appeared to pause before the bulk of a tank stand, his head twisting this way and that as he surveyed his shadowy beat. For a long moment Ketchell feared he would turn and head in his direction. Instead the man finally coughed, adjusted his hat and moved off downslope to vanish beyond the corrals.

Floyd slow-counted to one hundred, then followed.

Despite his calm he was still aware of a cold sweat across his brow by the time he'd returned safely to his starting point some quarter-hour later.

At one stage he had actually stood a mere hundred yards from the massive tallowood steps leading up to the immense front gallery of the main ranchhouse, where doubtless all the Amadors slept – Ethan, Rod and Earl.

He'd stood there in total darkness for seemingly an age, breathing silently through his mouth with the forefinger of his right hand caressing pistol trigger before an interior light went on, at which he'd instantly retreated.

Then went reconnoitring.

Aware he could meet trouble head-on any moment, he nonetheless had darted, flitted and light-footed his way completely around the enemy's bristling headquarters over some half an hour in which time he'd identified the position of one well-placed lookout after another.

His first impression had been the headquarters was undermanned. That was certainly unexpected, yet struck him as encouraging. But following his risky scout operation he now realized the very opposite was the case.

The real extent of the security he detected told him clearly that Slash K East was on a war footing tonight! It also suggested that, for all his outward indifference to Ketchell's return, the most powerful and dangerous man in the county might be actually afraid.

Sleeving his brow, he relived those individual moments of danger when he had detected in turn . . . a rustle of movement upon a shadowed rooftop . . . the glint of light upon gunmetal from a recessed barn doorway . . . picked up the sound of a suppressed cough from a pathway he'd riskily flitted across just minutes earlier. . . .

Yet he had survived it all to stand now motionless in back of a pin oak, finally facing up to the reality that the Amador heartland was impregnable.

Slash K East ranch was a bristling fortress!

Was he the reason why?

That was the only explanation that made sense of all this security. Or was it? He was only too well aware the Amadors could boast more enemies than Judas Iscariot. He listed them. There was the score and more of small beef ranchers whose entire futures might depend on securing a Paradise beef contract; the rustler gangs from all over for whom Slash K had proven a powerful temptation over the years; the towners and everyday citizens who'd suffered at the Amadors' hands over the years.

No shortage of enemies to explain these iron

defences, that was plain. But he still went with his first notion that he was the reason for the massive defences encountered tonight. Initially it had seemed the clan had ignored his return. Now every instinct suggested Amador must always have suspected he would ride back to revenge some day what had been done to him that bloody Friday with a blacksnake whip. . . .

He was jolted alert by the awareness that a heavy band of cloud had come in from beyond the great house, throwing all beneath it into Stygian gloom. He took advantage of it to move. By the time it passed away into the south, a lone horseman had cleared the eastern border and was following the trail back to town.

He'd wanted to kill tonight. That was not possible. Yet the venture was anything but a waste of time. Now he knew exactly what he was up against. He'd had to see with his own eyes that the mansion was still there, that his enemy lay within, and that it would be harder than he'd ever expected to reach him, yet possible. Anything was possible providing a man came armed with enough hatred, and he had assessed his hate over the years like a vengeful King Midas.

While his scarred back ached and ached as it had not done in a long time. . . .

By the time dawn touched the eastern skyline he was long gone and far out along the broad main trail back to the town. He planned on having hash browns and coffee for breakfast. And maybe one small swig of John T. for the strangely bitter taste in his mouth.

*

Heavy and sombre in their dark clothing and the awesome physical power of their large and powerful bodies, the Amador brothers sat across the desk from the lawman and watched him sweat nervously before they were ready to speak.

It was mid morning two days later and Al Yearly appeared anything but well rested. The town had been relatively quiet for a change, but the sheriff found this in no way reassuring. A rip-roaring brawl between towners and cowboys might have relieved the tensions and convinced him that everything was normal, enabling him to sleep a little better. But there had been scarce any violence lately, and that only served to sharpen the feeling he had that something wasn't right. As a consequence he wasn't sleeping, and it showed.

'So?' he said at last, when it seemed the heavy silence might be indefinitely prolonged. 'Something I can do for you, gents?'

No response. The Amadors continued to sit five feet apart in varnished jailhouse chairs, exuding both arrogance and the natural authority invested in them by both name and position.

It was enough to give any honest badgeman the cold sweats.

Only when good and ready did Rod, older of the two, break the silence.

'He's still here, we hear tell.'

'He?' Yearly looked from one big slab of a face to the other. 'Oh . . . reckon you mean—'

'That son of a bitch Ketchell is still walking around here like he owns the place!' Earl growled. 'And you ain't done one mortal thing about it. Just tell me one thing, Yearly. That tin star on your vest there. Why in hell do you think you get paid for wearing that thing?'

'Well, I, er—'

'To do your job, is what, damnit!' Rod cut him off. 'But are you doing it where this man is concerned? He comes back after all this time, everybody's speculating on why he returned and we reckon you'd have to know the answer to that as well as anybody. To raise hell, is what! Kill the old man. So, when do you plan to lock the bastard up, shoot him down or move him on?'

Yearly was sweating. He was a tolerably tough peace officer and not afraid of these two, but was intimidated by the power they represented. If Ethan Amador genuinely wanted him fired by the council, then he could kiss his star goodbye right now. He had a wife and kids.

'But he hasn't broken any law,' he protested. 'I can't arrest a man unless—'

He broke off as both men rose together. They appeared big as houses.

'We're here to tell you the old man expects something to be done, and fast,' Rod said tonelessly, picking his hat up off the lawman's desk. 'Get rid of Ketchell or the old man will surely get rid of you. That plain enough to suit— Sheriff?'

'But—' Yearly began, but his voice trailed away. For they were already gone, tramping across the sagging planking of his verandah, foundation supports creaking in protest beneath their great weight.

'If there's anybody in this county who should be got rid of . . . it's you two and your father, by God!' the sheriff of Liberty said bitterly. But said it very softly.

CHAPTER 5

THE CLAN

He was leaning against an upright in the shade of the post office porch with a freshly lighted cigarette jutting from his teeth when he sighted the badge-man approaching. Ketchell's expression did not change but something hardened inside him. He'd been expecting to confront Yearly ever since his arrival, yet up until now the lawman had barely exchanged the time of day. That suited Floyd Ketchell, although he didn't expect it to last. For Yearly had a job to do, just as he had his.

Up close he realized how little the sheriff of Liberty had changed over the years. Pound or two heavier, maybe a little greyer. But the man still had the same stare – cold, implacable, suspicious. Nonetheless, this badge toter had survived in a mighty hard job in a turbulent town. You might not like him, and few did, yet he managed to maintain a tolerable level of law and order within the city limits, while wisely leaving much of whatever went on out across the rangelands to the beef barons.

Ketchell took a deep drag on his cigarette and gusted smoke above the sheriff's head as the man halted in the street below him.

'Howdy, Yearly.'

The lawman folded arms across narrow chest and squinted. Three miners passing by slowed down to glance back curiously, then continued on their way. Ketchell's return had sent out shock waves that continued to ripple. But with days drifting by without serious trouble, most folks were beginning to relax, the optimists amongst them actually opining that maybe his homecoming would not prove a trigger for bloodshed after all.

One man who fervently wished he could believe that was the sheriff.

'Howdy, Floyd. Ahh . . . saw you coming out of the attorney's the other day. Got some legal problems, have you?'

'I don't have any problems.'

'If you had would you tell me?'

'No.'

Yearly flushed. 'Five years sure ain't improved your manners any.'

'Something on your mind, Sheriff?'

'What do you think, mister? You hit my town and suddenly every man and his dog is walking on eggshells. Did you know that Petey Doyle at the Golden Hawk is laying odds that there will be gunplay between you and the Amadors before the end of the week?'

'Is that what they're thinking? Well, I guess

anything's possible if the sun keeps shining and the creeks don't rise.'

The lawman stiffened.

'Are you being smart with me, boy? On account if you are, then you should be reminded that I'm still the law in this town and I've got the power to throw anybody in jail I want. Either that or have them move on if I believe they might cause trouble. Well, just the way you're acting right now gives me a real strong whiff of trouble, son, so I'm inviting you to move on—'

'Drop it!'

Yearly paled. 'What did you say?'

Ketchell jumped down lightly into the street. He was the same height as the peace officer but somehow in that moment appeared both taller and far more dangerous.

'Don't you tell me to do anything, Yearly. Not now and not ever!'

The lawman was shaken but managed to hold his ground, even mustered a little defiance.

'You will heed me, Ketchell. I am sheriff of this town and you—'

'*Sheriff?*' Ketchell made the word sound ugly. He leaned forwards, transfixing the older man with eyes like drills. 'Just what breed of sheriff do you really claim to be? Or could I be wrong about you?' His tone was caustic. 'Maybe that day when they tried to murder me in front of the whole town, *Sheriff* Yearly wasn't really locked away in his own jailhouse hiding behind the door like folks said? Maybe he was out here on the streets warning the

Amadors to quit breaking the law, and for the old man to get shot of that whip of his? Hell! I'll wager you were doing all those things but I was just too dumb to realize it.'

Al Yearly wilted visibly before the attack. Lines of fear and uncertainty gouged the man's face and he was compelled to take a backward step away from those accusing eyes.

'I wanted to do something that day, Floyd. Honest. As God is my judge I—'

The sheriff broke off when he was brushed roughly aside and Ketchell went striding off along the street.

He was angry as he walked.

The hell with Yearly!

But at least he would not have to worry about the badgeman bracing him again, he predicted. He'd taken him on and the man came apart like something made of wet straw. That was something well put behind. For common sense warned that before he was through here he could find himself up against the worst kind of trouble coming at him from a dozen different directions. If so, he could well do without the law strengthening the enemy ranks.

Reaching the Glass Slipper and ignoring the curious stares of porch loafers, he mounted the steps and shouldered through the swinging doors.

Turk Henry greeted him warily as he ordered whiskey, and Jenny Prentiss quit the company of a hard rock miner to come join him at the bar. The three chatted quietly together for a time in the big quiet room with its windows opened to the morning, sipping their drinks.

A spell later the batwings banged open and two big men came in and made for the bar, both wearing smiles that looked pasted on. Ketchell realized belatedly he'd been half expecting the Amador brothers to show up today.

'Well, well, it sure is like the good old days having a drink with young Floyd here, ain't it?' Rod Amador declared boisterously.

'Surely, surely.' Earl's grin was more a grimace. 'Still hard to believe you've been away five long years, Floyd.'

Seated opposite the brothers at a corner table in the Glass Slipper's main bar-room with a solid wall at his back, Floyd Ketchell hefted the bottle of John T. Smith whiskey and topped up all three glasses.

The pair watched him too steadily and it was hard to keep his features blank. They were trying to create the impression they'd been friendly once, whereas about the only contact he'd ever had with either in the old days had involved bare knuckles in vicious saloon brawls.

Looking back, it was difficult to recall if he'd won or lost those fights. Of course, winning or losing had been of no real importance to easy-going Floyd Ketchell in those times. It was not until he'd spent three months of agony recovering from his flogging that he realized he was transformed into a man who would never permit himself to lose with fists, words or roaring six-shooters ever again.

Naturally the Amador brothers had also changed plenty over the years. The old man's genes showed even more visibly in both men now. They had mutated into powerful presences with a new force and confidence which he suspected had come to full flower since their father was restricted to a wheelchair.

He supposed Ethan Amador was still the dominant figure out there on the K East. Yet the old man's loss of mobility would have to be a severe handicap, while his older sons were the breed to take quick advantage of any weakness in anybody. That was the way they were made.

The conversation focused for a time on the 'good old days' which in reality they had never shared. But eventually the stilted talk petered out into an uneasy silence. Earl's attention drifted to the girls behind the bar while the older brother sat in silence and fiddled absently with the heavy gold watch chain slung across his flat middle.

Yet the pair was anything but relaxed, and instinct warned Ketchell their meeting was not accidental. Nor was it over.

It was Rod who finally broke the silence in his typically abrupt manner.

'Mind telling us what brought you back?'

'Yeah, I mind.'

Colour stained the man's taut cheekbones. 'Folks are saying that—'

'Quit blowing on the fur and get to the hide. What do you want with me?'

They were angry but did not stalk off. After studying him for maybe a full minute, Rod Amador leaned back and dragged on his cheroot.

'Heard you had a run-in with our kid sister?'

'Guess you could call it that.'

Amador's smile was more a grimace

'Changed a lot, our sister. But I reckon you would have noticed that?'

'Mebbe.'

'Everything's changed hereabouts since you been gone,' Earl weighed in.

'Damn right,' Ketchell's tone was sarcastic. 'Why, before I left there was scarce any back-shooting, hired gunpackers or regular buryings like they say there is today.'

Stung by his sarcasm the two stared at him stonily across the big table, weighing him with their eyes, probing for a weakness.

Eventually Rod spoke up with fake heartiness. 'Well, we've sure heard plenty about you since you quit Liberty, yes sir! Why, only the other day Earl here showed me a bit in a newspaper about you shooting a badman name of Clint Hogue down in Mexico. Paper said this Hogue was something of a two-gun terror until you put him on ice. Amazing how you've come on. I mean, before you left here you were no more than a passable hand with a six-gun – hell of a good wrangler, but just average with a cutter.'

His cold Amador eyes dropped to the .38 jutting from the holster on his hip. 'Yessir, sure is remarkable. . . .'

Ketchell reckoned he was catching their drift by

this. But he had no intention of helping them get to where they wanted to go. He simply sat sipping whiskey in silence and reflecting on how much he hated them both. But one thing he was not guilty of, was taking them lightly. Anything but. Looking through the prism of his hard-won experience with the world, he saw both were in their full prime and were most likely posing a threat to their father's brutal authority out there on the ranch these days.

This was a vital factor to take into consideration for someone bent on revenge to consider. He reckoned Ethan Amador would have to be proud of his two first-born, even if he was never likely to admit it. Using the same ready reckoning, he guessed Tara and Johnny had not come up to the old man's expectations and had been treated accordingly.

His thoughts briefly turned to Tara. She was still acting hostile and aggressive whenever their paths crossed, but maybe he was beginning to understand why now. In cutting himself off from everything here it must seem he'd been punishing her along with the rest of her family.

Proof of this lay in the fact that she and young Johnny had been kicked off Slash K East when banished to the level of poor kinfolk out on K West.

His train of thought broke when Rod began tapping the table with a thick, blunt finger, causing a little drumming sound that held an almost ominous rhythm.

'Yessir, you sure are a big name in the South-West by now, Floyd,' the man remarked quietly. 'Which means, no doubt, you could hire yourself out for serious money?'

'Top dollar.'

The flat brown eyes met his. It was like looking through the window of an empty house.

'What is top money these days?'

'Don't you now?' Floyd said. 'I figured that with you fellers hiring guntippers all over you'd—'

'Tara is the one hiring guns,' Earl cut in sharply. 'All we've been doing on Slash K East as troubles seem to pile up worse and worse by the day now, has been hiring the odd extra shooter who can use a gun as well as he punch cows. It's called self protection.'

'But we're finding that ain't enough,' stated Rod. 'Since Ralls and his rannies hit town and signed on with Tara and Johnny, that is. Matter of fact we've got a feeling we're losing ground in this family feud – like you might call it. So tell me, Floyd, what are they paying out for a genuine class shootist these days?'

'I've worked for two hundred a week in New Mexico.'

The brothers traded glances. Ketchell was talking big money. He realized how serious they were when Rod finally sighed, and said, 'That's a lot of dollars, by God. . . .' A pause, then, 'But, OK, mister, guess we're ready to meet it.'

He managed to appear surprised. 'You fellers offering me gun work?'

'What does it sound like?' snapped Rod, sounding more his old self.

'Sorry.'

'What do you mean – sorry?'

Ketchell rose. 'I've hired my Colt for various reasons at times. But money was never one.'

'Let me guess whyso, mister.' Rod Amador suddenly looked dangerous. 'Are you telling us that instead of doing it for *dinero*, you turned yourself into a guntipper just so that someday you'd feel big enough to come back here and gun down the old man?'

Silence. The two stared at him fixedly. Ketchell met their looks with hooded eyes, not wanting them to see his hate too clearly.

'Kill Ethan?' he said with fake incredulity. 'Biggest and toughest old bastard in a hundred miles with two strapping sons and twenty gunhands to protect him? I'd need to be Bill Hickok as twins and I still wouldn't stand a hope in hell of nailing him, not even if I wanted to.'

This was just talk. Yet the reality was that Ethan Amador did appear as safe as any man could be out there in his castle beef had built.

Which could be the main reason the old bastard was still breathing.

Slash K East was a fortress with the headquarters guarded by gunmen day and night. If he was to get his man it might have to be well away from the K headquarters – or if he could raise a small army. Which probably added up to the harsh fact that the man was likely safe as the Bank of America right now.

And he wondered, not for the first time, if that vengeful goal that had driven him so hard for so long would ever be realized.

The brothers rose together in silence.

In an instant they had become total strangers. He could feel the cold heat of their hatred – and beneath the table his lethal fingertips touched the scrolled butt plate of his .38 – best friend he had in life.

He did not relax until they turned broad backs and crossed to the long bar to slap the mahogany for service. Floyd sipped his drink and watched them talking and gesticulating from beneath his hooded eyelids.

Eventually they returned to loom before his table like two pillars of salt.

'We'll put our cards on the table, Ketchell,' stated Rod. 'What's happening out here on the range right now is that the beef market is getting crowded. So much so we're even in open competition with our own sister. Tara knows it and damn me if she's not putting up a real fight. You know? Kowtowing to the beef buyers and all – even flirting with that beef agent, Tumbrille, from down south, where the big clients are these days. The time could fast come when we might have to turn mean and treat her like any other enemy.' A pause. 'You following so far?'

He nodded. The brothers had never been complex. He reckoned it was easy enough to figure where this conversation was leading.

'OK,' chimed in Earl, leaning a paw on the table and lowering his voice. 'We'll be dead straight. Me and Rod and the old man are all of one mind agreeing that there's no way we aim to miss out on any part of that big contract with the beef agents from Paradise who we've been working on hard for quite a spell now. Simply can't risk that falling through. Won't. Sis won't listen to reason any more. She's sweet-talked her way in with the Paradise's top beef agent, and if we don't do something about it then K East is going to miss out. And that is where you and Ralls come in.'

He pricked his ears. 'Ralls?'

'Tara hired that gunner just days after the last time we roughed her up some,' Rod admitted unashamedly 'She figured we might get to play a lot rougher than that even, so she ran herself into debt to import Ralls and his bunch to protect her. Sure, we could still roll right over K West if it came to gunplay. But why should we risk honest hands against a guntipper like Ralls? That's bad enough, like you might figure. But just say that Judas woman was to sweet talk a gunner like you into backing her as well, why we might wind up with the odds in the family war swinging her way.'

Earl's eyes resembled twin stones. 'We can't sit back and let that happen. We won't.'

Ketchell nodded slowly. Now he understood the set-up only too well. If he was shocked to hear men talk of a range war against their own flesh and blood, he gave no sign.

He said quietly. 'Still not available.'

They stood before him shoulder to shoulder, a menacing wall of humanity.

'In that case, ride out, Ketchell,' Rod ordered. 'That is the best advice you'll ever get, mister.'

'I left a town before I was ready to go once,' he replied evenly. 'This town. I don't mean to do it again, not for you and not for anybody. Savvy?'

They stood stonily silent for a moment. Ketchell narrowed his eyes and pictured Rod Amador transformed into his own father – standing over him with a bloodied whip dangling from clenched fist.

Rod was first to blink. With a vicious curse he spun and went striding, forcing his brother to break into a trot to catch him up. The pair shouldered out through the batwings together and Ketchell was left with the feeling that the next time they met could well be over roaring sixguns.

It was a good dream Martens was having. He'd quit the county and was living it up in Mesa City with no less than three blonde dancers who were not one lick better than they should be, and who seemed intent on having their way with him in the snug back room of the Golden West Saloon, whether he liked it or not. But before he could surrender and maybe risk dying of pure pleasure, he must do something about his right foot. Something kept banging against the sole, and when he frowned and struggled to figure out what it was, this caused him to jolt awake and find himself gaping up at a tall lean figure silhouetted against the moon.

He blinked foolishly then gasped in pain when Ralls drove the toe of his flashy riding boot into his foot again, was struggling to rise when an openhanded slap to the side of the head sent him sprawling in the hillside grass.

'On your feet, you bum!'

Martens stumbled to his feet, wild anger gripping his face now. For he was a tough gunner from Kansas who though well aware of Ralls's deadly rep was still no man to be pushed around.

He gripped gun handle as he sleeved his mouth with the back of his hand.

'You'll do something like that once too often, Ralls. So I was catching forty winks. So what? I didn't sign on here to freeze my arse off keeping watch for nobody who shows up. None of us did. Ask Slim or Buddy if—'

'You'll do just what I say, pilgrim. What I told you to do was to stand post and watch the K East border until midnight when you get relieved. You want to do that or get paid up?'

The hardcase spat to show his defiance, yet gave ground even so. He liked riding with Ralls, even if he was both ornery and dangerous.

'Just make sure I'm relieved . . . that's if you can concentrate on anything but that skirt we're riding for,' he was game enough to fire back.

'Keep looking for trouble and you'll sure find it, bonehead!' Ralls shot back in turn. Then strode to his horse, vaulted into the saddle and headed down for the homestead at the gallop.

She was still up when he arrived, soberly studying her face in a small square of mirror where she sat at the round table in the front room. The rest of the K West headquarters was asleep save for two slow-pacing gunmen outside. Ralls whipped off his hat and waited to be acknowledged. When that did not happen he hurled his hat aside and crossed to the table.

'I'm back!'

'Wonderful.'

Emotions chased one another over the gunman's hawk features – desire, doubt, anger, uncertainty. Accustomed to authority and respect, Jubal Ralls was finding his pride and status continually challenged here where he was second in command to the mistress of K West herself. His men always toed the line with him, while young Johnny Amador mostly avoided him, which suited them both. So he felt he had every male on the place bluffed, while the sole female often treated him like poor trash.

'Look, Tara—'

She rose swiftly with cat-like grace, snapping her fingers right beneath his nose.

'Don't start,' she warned. 'I've had a long day and I don't intend to wind it up listening to your bitching or complaining. I'll just make one thing plain, mister. If you don't like the way things are run here – there's the door. You are good at what you do, but you don't know your place and you have far too much to say. Now, did you have something in particular you wanted to say, mister?'

The colour drained from the gunman's face.

'By God you never talked to me this way before he showed up. He changed every fragging thing here, didn't he? Ketchell, I mean. You claim you hate him because he came back to get the old man, yet any time a man says one word against him you act like—'

101

'Good night!'

'What?'

'You heard. See me at breakfast. And if you are still running off at the mouth like a colicky mule then I'll pay you all out and you are off K West.'

For a moment it seemed as if he might strike her. He was riled enough to do it. Yet she stood before him without fear, radiating that steely composure which everyone had grown familiar with ever since she became mistress of the K West Ranch.

'All right,' he got out at length, 'I'm going. But if Ketchell should show and—'

'I believe you said you were going?'

Moments later she was alone, the room still vibrating from the door slamming on his way out. Tara Amador smiled cynically, wearily. Then she shrugged and started for her room, feeling she had won again.

Only in her room which she shared with no-one, did she let the tears go. Here, every night, she thought of the other half of her riven family, and what they might do to herself and her brother if she let down her defences for even a moment. And before sleeping, as always, thought of Floyd Ketchell – another man who caused her to weep, but for very different reasons.

CHAPTER 6

ONE VIOLENT NIGHT

Tara Amador was welcome most any place she went – with the exception of her family home. She had always been attractive, strong-willed, and some might say more than a little headstrong and outspoken. But she had grit and charm in abundance and seemed fearless by towners' standards, and therefore was widely admired in a place where independent young women were rare.

That night she was at the Golden Nugget Café on Wylde Street with two women friends and brother Johnny and his girl. And with troubles on her mind.

'What is it, honey?' a friend asked as they raised pre-supper drinks, with most male eyes in the place roaming their way. 'Or can we guess?'

They meant her family, Tara knew. The entire county was aware of their constant conflicts and troubles by this. She shrugged the question off and changed the subject, but her frown remained.

There was reason for her mood tonight. The beef agent from Paradise had contacted her upon his arrival to set up a meeting to discuss the all-important beef deal. She believed she was well prepared for this, although it was anything but simple or straightforward. For should K East hear of Tumbrille's visit, as they must, she could not be sure how they might react.

She turned at a touch on her shoulder, glanced up to see Ralls standing there, scowling.

'What?' she said.

The gunman gestured. 'Logan just told me he sighted your old boyfriend outside. . . .'

'So?'

'What if he comes in? You want I should throw him out?'

'No, I don't.' She rose sharply from her chair and drew the gunman to one side. 'Look, Jubal, your job is to watch out for me and keep alert for any sign of trouble from Slash K East. Floyd isn't part of your job. And just because I fight with him whenever I see him doesn't make him my enemy.'

'You sure about that?'

'Damnit, just do as I say, will you?'

She'd raised her voice. Her table stared as Jubal Ralls flushed. The handsome gunman seemed ready to go on with it, but changed his mind and testily returned to his two partners in the far corner.

'Honestly!' Tara said, resuming her seat. 'Now, what were we discussing, girls?'

'Floyd Ketchell,' one replied.

'What?' Tara snapped. Then turned her head as the eatery doors opened and Ketchell himself strolled in looking freshly shaved, bathed and togged out in some flash western tailoring.

He paused on sighting the group, removed his hat and approached.

Tara Amador's reaction was interesting for her friends to observe. Firstly she appeared annoyed, then began to smile, yet next swore under her breath. 'What does a person have to do to enjoy a quiet night in this stupid town?' she hissed.

'Evening, ladies.' Ketchell removed his hat and stood by her chair. The ghost of a smile. Last time they'd crossed paths she'd accused him of wanting to shoot her father. 'Beginning or finishing, Tara?'

'I'm sure I don't know what business that could be of yours, Floyd Ketchell. But if you must know, I just this moment decided I am not hungry after all . . . so if you will excuse me, girls?'

The women stared as she rose swiftly and took her shawl from the back of her chair, which she then held out for Ketchell to drape over her shoulders.

It was his turn to be surprised. Then from the corner of his eye he glimpsed Jubal Ralls threading his way through the tables towards them, jaw tight and eyes glittering.

'Don't start anything!' Tara warned him. 'I know how to handle Jubal.'

She proved this with just a few sharp words which saw Jubal Ralls turn pale with anger. Yet for the second time in one short night, the deadly guntipper found himself forced to backwater. He shot a bullet stare at Ketchell then swung away, glitter-eyed and tense.

By which time Tara had steered Floyd Ketchell out the side doors and down the steps, still holding his arm in a firm grip, as though she really meant it.

They started off along the lamplit plankwalk.

'How stupid was that?' she hissed, disentangling her arm. 'I'd been looking forward to a nice night with my friends for weeks, and you knew Ralls would be with me! You don't contact me for days on end, then you bob up just when you knew you would cause the most upset and—'

'How does Mrs Doolin's sound?'

'What? What are you talking about?'

'Well, you must be hungry. And that little fat momma whips up the best—'

She halted on a dime. 'You think I'd eat with you after—'

'This is important,' he cut in. 'I had to talk to you. I couldn't wait until we just chanced to meet.'

She studied him and some of the annoyance left her face. She realized he was as serious as she had ever seen him.

'Break it to me gently,' she said in her wry way. 'In the meantime, what is the specialty of the house at Mrs Doolin's?'

'Horse,' he grinned.

'My favorite,' she laughed, and took him by the arm.

'So,' Ethan Amador rumbled, turning his whiskey

glass slowly in a huge hand, 'what you claimed couldn't happen, has just happened? Is that what you're telling me?'

The brothers stood before the wheelchair with the early morning light flooding through big windows overlooking valley and river. Out on the range the small dots of riders could be seen mustering stock for the inspection. In close upon the home acres heavily armed hands moved about on their slow, watchful rounds, eternally guarding the compound and watchful for any trouble that may still expected to come.

The morning was cool and someone was playing piano upstairs in the great house. Yet the music was not reaching down as far as the vast deck room where three breakfasts were slowly going cold upon an oaken table.

The brothers traded silent stares.

They'd been ordered to furnish the old man a complete report on all recent events of significance. This included the fact that their sister and Ketchell had shared a two-hour supper in Liberty the previous night, and were later sighted strolling along Main Street.

The news hit like a bomb. Due to earlier fiery clashes between Ketchell and their sister and daughter since his return, the K East had shelved much of the concern they'd had that the ill-starred romance between the two from years ago might be revived.

Word that they'd been together again was something Ethan Amador didn't welcome on the same morning that had brought other bad news concerning their pending deal with Paradise. He'd received a note informing that beef agent Tom Tumbrille would be in the region shortly to inspect both Slash Ks prior to awarding the big beef supply contract for the workmen at the iron ore mine down south.

Up until that point Amador had not even known lowly K West was in contention for the contract.

'That treacherous girl,' he growled darkly, staring out through the great plate glass windows, 'has been a grave disappointment to me. . . .'

His voice trailed away. The brothers traded glances over his massive grey head. Their expressions were blank. Neither regarded sister and kid brother as blood kin any longer, but rather as irritants and potential obstacles to their ambition to rule K East between them soon. That would mean no old man or kinfolk hampering their big ambitions. The two confidently expected that following that final big dust-up between Tara and the old man, the two junior Amadors would simply remain out there on their lousy piece of dirt and eventually simply drop out of their lives. Permanently.

But that was before Ralls.

Tara was proving herself far tougher and more capable than any dumb female had a right to be, in their eyes. Marooned out there on hard-scrabble K West with their kid brother, she hadn't folded up meekly but borrowed from the bank, improved her stock out of sight and had even laid out hard money to hire a deadly gunman with three back-ups.

K East accused sister and daughter of suspicion

and mistrust. But she was not through yet. Her next independent decision was to make contact with agent Tom Tumbrille down in Paradise and persuade him to inspect and consider *her* K West cattle as well on his pending visit to K East.

This had sent the old man into one of his towering rages that had house staff cowering in the cellars and cowhands looking for safer places to work.

Somehow the family weathered that storm. But this new information that Tara might have patched up differences with Floyd Ketchell came like an outright declaration of war.

'She's teetering on the brink,' Ethan announced in a suddenly stronger voice, swinging his chair about to put the view at his back. 'Hiring Ralls was like throwing down the gauntlet to me personal, but nothing I couldn't handle. However, if she's planning to enlist that Ketchell scum for any reason, then by God and by Judas I won't be sitting back just to let that happen.'

'What do you want us to do about it, Dad?' Rod asked.

'When I figure that I'll let you know. Now get the hell out!'

The pair quit the room and the old man wheeled across to his liquor cabinet. With glass in hand he turned to gaze broodingly out over his empire of men, cattle and grass for a long time in total silence.

And deeply regretted the fact that he hadn't killed Ketchell when he'd had the chance.

'I could do it now,' he muttered. And thought yet

again, 'I should have finished the bastard while I had the chance. . . .'

He sounded as strong as ever. Yet throwing the raw liquor down his throat he felt it again somewhere deep in his bowels . . . that sensation of waning powers and creeping fear which he alone knew had infected him the day and the hour Ketchell first showed.

He'd once done that boy a massive injury, expected him to die as a result, never anticipated he might ever return packing a gun loaded with hate. . . .

The edifice that had been the king of Slash K East was crumbling from within, and only he knew it.

How he would have been boosted up to know that at that very moment, somebody else, potentially as ruthless as himself, was not only making plans to kill Ketchell but was close to putting them into action.

They had him surrounded before he even suspected he could be in danger. And even as he hauled the hammerhead to a halt he realized they must have been waiting to ambush him when next he showed up along this desolate patch of K West backtrail.

His hand wrapped round gunbutt. But he did not draw. Not with naked six-guns lined up on him in the starlight, he didn't. He'd only glimpsed three of them at a distance in Liberty once or twice, but Jubal Ralls was familiar.

Ugly Rufe McCluskey smirked at him in the thick

silence, cocking the weapon in his hand with a click, then spitting into the tall grass.

'Lose your way, hero?' the hardcase smirked. 'Or mebbe I got it wrong? Mebbe it ain't old man Amador you're laying for after all?' He snapped his fingers. 'Hey! Just had me a sharp notion. It's the old man's *daughter* you're looking to shoot up . . . seeing this is the back trail to K West. Ain't that how it is?'

With both hands resting motionless upon his saddle pommel, Ketchell ignored the man. He was watching Ralls. He rated McCluskey and the others of the bunch as second-raters. But Ralls was class. Might even prove to be the same breed as himself – so he'd sensed from the start. Gunslinger for sure. But maybe even killer?

Ralls pushed his flash horse closer, starlight dusting hat and shoulders.

'Lose your way, Ketchell?' His manner was cold. 'You know, I understood you came back to the county to settle something with Ethan Amador. But like Rufe says, this old track only leads downhill to Tara's front door. Now how does that figure?'

Ketchell made no response. He was figuring what the situation could mean, how great his danger. Ralls had chosen this spot well. It was remote and isolated. But his men were bunched far too close together should it come to gunplay. He calmly decided to kill Ralls first should it come to a showdown. The man might well be fast, yet he still believed he had the edge. Blast the guntipper. Ride like hell. Trust to luck.

If it came to that.

'All right, Ralls – what's the play?'

'Can't understand a smart man like you riding about careless in enemy country, Ketchell,' Ralls replied. 'Or should that read . . . former enemy? I mean, just yesterday Tara couldn't say enough bad about you, yet this morning when she was heading back out to the spread from town she seemed to be dancing on air. How do you figure a female, Ketchell? Maybe I could use some good tips?'

The gunman's eyes glittered cold and Ketchell wasn't unsure any longer. This was all about Tara. He'd either read Ralls wrong or simply hadn't realized the gunman could be interested in her.

This showed plain enough now; it was written all over Ralls' good-looking mug.

He nodded slowly.

'I'll give you the best tip you ever had in your life, Ralls. Get the hell out of my way or I'll shift you. That clear enough for you?'

The air was electric as Jubal Ralls straightened in his saddle. Watching the man to the exclusion of the others, Ketchell knew gunsmoke was close, was ready as he'd ever been to deal with whatever might come.

'You're not seeing Tara, Ketchell! Not now and not never. Hear me? You screwed her life up once, now you're looking to do it again. But things are different now. She's got someone to look out for her – quite a few someones if you just look around. . . .'

Heads nodded in agreement. Ketchell remained

a picture of icy calm. Sure, the odds stank. Yet it was far from the first time he'd been in a situation like this. He didn't know what lay between Ralls and Tara. All he was sure of was that he wanted to see her tonight, and he meant to do that or go down shooting.

It was at that explosive moment, with gunsmoke so close a man could almost smell it, Jubal Ralls made one vital mistake. He flicked a glance to his right where ugly McCluskey sat his sorrel mare. Just one look, but it rang all the warning bells in Ketchell's skull.

He ducked low and drew as McCluskey's six-shooter cleared oiled leather with a sibilant hiss.

Ketchell's right hand came up filled with .38 as his heels slammed horsehide. The animal surged forward before McCluskey's gun thundered. It was a wild shot but Ketchell's bullet hammered home, smashing into the man's shoulder and belting him backwards out of his saddle causing the riders in back of him to jerk-rein away in wild confusion.

There was yelling and shooting in the moonlight but already Ketchell's ugly horse was hitting full stride to go rocketing away downslope. He jerk-reined the animal off the trail and flashed through the timber, ignoring the rising clamour thundering behind, intent only on speed and horsemanship.

He was soon back in familiar country. And when he figured he'd led them far enough, he simply vanished again. From that point he followed three separate trails to confuse pursuit, paused only long enough to build a cigarette and then unerringly cut a track that ran south by south-west.

Twenty minutes later he glimpsed the welcoming lights of K West headquarters through the oaks.

She was brushing her hair before a full-length mirror when she suddenly felt her spine tingle. Dressed only in underclothes before her mirror, and without a whisper of sound to alert her, Tara Amador knew even before she turned that she was no longer alone in her room at headquarters in the middle of the night. She was unfazed and almost regal as she turned unhurriedly to face her intruder.

'I didn't hear you knock.'

He almost laughed. It was long past midnight, he was half out of breath, soaked in sweat, had lost his hat and knew he must resemble some kind of wild man from the woods.

The only reason he didn't laugh was that he was still angry – and maybe halfway suspicious.

He sleeved his forehead and came deeper into the room. Romance was far from his mind yet he still could not ignore how lovely she looked standing there, silently indicating with a gesture her robe draped over the back of a red plush chair.

He handed the garment across and she took it without comment. Another woman would have demanded to know just what in hell he was doing in her boudoir in the middle of the night uninvited. But Tara Amador was not just another woman. She had been reared in a house filled with tensions and anger and an eternal undercurrent of violence.

She'd grown to womanhood in the company of four men, three of whom were undeniably arrogant, ruthless and cruel. Only the fourth, her youngest sibling, had always been close and loving. Somehow she had succeeded in fashioning her own life here with Johnny. And if she had half forgotten how much in love she had been once – seemingly an eternity ago – her nocturnal caller had not.

Ketchell had come to this plain house at this odd hour despite all dangers and risks. He was relieved to have made it, yet was still not certain why he'd had to come. Yet when he saw her looking as he did now, he realized he did know the reason. Of course he did! It had almost slipped his mind following the violence and the hell-for-leather night ride, was all.

'I needed to talk,' he stated.

'Well, we can talk in the kitchen, and have some coffee as well.'

He followed her through, conscious of the quiet. 'Johnny around?'

'Out courting,' she said, punching up the fire in the pot-belly. 'There's a girl at the Double Forty. They're so cute together.'

'I recall folks saying that about us once,' he replied, taking a chair at the table.

She turned to face him directly. 'What's on your mind, Floyd? Last time I saw you, you were almost light-hearted, but tonight you seem . . . different. Very different, I would think.' She frowned. 'Why are you smiling?'

'Guess it's because I'd forgotten how you could always read me like fine print . . . back in the old days.'

'Then . . . something is wrong?'

He was as sober as a hanging judge as he stared down at the mug of coffee she brought across to the table. He nodded and tasted it, deep creases cutting his brows as he looked up.

'Yeah.' He was silent for a moment, searching for words. Then he leaned back. 'You were right about me, of course. I came back to put your father in the ground. Well, tonight I decided either to do it right away or admit I didn't have the guts. I've been out to K East a dozen times, and I've always known the the layout like the back of my hand. I reckon I could still find my way in there past all that security and give Ethan six of the best and then get out with a whole skin anytime I wanted. . . .'

He paused and met her eyes. 'Sure, it's ugly. But you wanted to know. . . .'

'Keep talking. So, what happened? How did you wind up here on K West instead?'

His expression underwent swift changes from wooden, through puzzled to confused. He rose sharply and commenced pacing the confines of the room, reliving one of the strangest days of his life . . . the day and the night that had changed everything. . . .

One week earlier. . . .

It was the heaviest rainfall of the season and he lay beneath it under a dripping shelf of stone less than a quarter mile from K East ranchhouse with field glasses pressed to his eyes.

A miserable Amador sentry hunched beneath a

116

tarpaulin a short distance below his position with no notion that the danger they had been half expecting for over two weeks was almost within spitting distance.

And out upon the covered decking with storm lamps lit to counter the gloom – looking larger than life in the magnification of his field glasses – a huge grey old man seated in a wheelchair.

It was the closest he'd come to the man he'd waited five years to kill . . . yet he belly-wriggled away through the mud and rain with his gun unfired to reach his sodden horse eventually and head back to the town.

Two hours later he stood dripping and pale in his hotel room.

It lay before him upon the table in the pool of light cast by the hanging lamp.

The gun.

It was an old familiar friend with its scrolled butt plates and elegant long barrel. It had saved his life many times over the violent years, had helped him live just how and where he might choose.

He'd built a great skill and a feared name with that good gun throughout the violent South-west, and it had never failed him nor he it, until today.

He could have shot and killed the man he hated with one bullet – believed he would likely have escaped unscathed in that rainstorm after the job was done – revenge accomplished.

But he couldn't.

For the man he'd watched through his glasses out there today was not a violent, arrogant bastard wielding a blacksnake whip, but a crumbling and clearly fearful old man, plainly sweating blood every day from the fear that he would come and kill him, no matter how many guns protected him.

He felt drained and directionless. But stronger than that was the realization that he was not the brutal killer he'd feared he could become, after all. Somehow, he'd learned how to forgive . . . and the first person he'd had to tell this to was the woman standing before him now.

He waited for her reaction to a story that even to his own ears had sounded strange in the telling. He didn't seem to breathe or feel until she suddenly brushed away a tear and came into his arms.

'I stood in my room with my shooter in hand telling mself to go get it done, get on my nag and ride away to, to enjoy the rest of my life in peace – finally at peace with the world. . . .'

'But you couldn't? Is that what you are telling me?'

'How . . . how did you guess?'

'Am I right, then?'

'Right. . . .'

His voice sounded strange even to his own ears. He circled the room with slow steps, staring at nothing.

In his mind he was back in the pouring rain with his gun in his fist willing himself to complete the task that had dominated his thoughts for five years.

Yet no matter how vividly he was able to revive memory of that day from hell here in Box Butte

County, with what clarity he feared might never leave him he could recall that pain and all those sleepless nights he'd spent conjuring up the final image of himelf standing victorious with a smoking gun over the huge riddled body sprawled at his feet – his heart told him he could never do it . . . so he forked his bronc to make that risky ride out to Slash K West.

'Then you're free at last, aren't you?'

The voice seemed to come from afar. He stared at her but there was no reading her expression. He knew how he'd hurt her. Hadn't written. Never stopped by to see if she needed him – as he now sensed she *had* done. Too caught up with his pain, his pride, his hate.

'If you could call it that,' he said, and she was reaching for him when they heard the horses in the yard.

The gun filled his hand as steps sounded on the gallery and Ralls strode into the room, tall, mean-eyed and .45 in hand.

'Tara!' the man panted. 'Get the hell away from that mongrel and I'll—'

'Don't be tiresome, Jubal,' Tara said calmly. 'And do put that pistol away. Now!'

'Damn you, Tara—' he began, but Ketchell cut him off.

'Do like the lady says, man. You went off half-cocked earlier tonight, so don't get to look dumb twice in the one day.'

Ralls swore viciously but broke off as McCluskey staggered in clutching a bloodied shoulder, his face the colour of old rope.

Ketchell stepped back and watched Tara take over. She called for hot water and bandages, calmly ordering angry men about with smooth authority, seemingly ignoring Ralls's angry glare and occasionally catching Ketchell's eye, and half nodding as if to say everything was all right.

And maybe it was – for her, he mused as he stepped out onto the porch to fashion a desperately needed Bull Durham. But for himself, he simply wasn't sure. He only knew that when the sun got up in the morning it would be a very different world from that which he had lived in for five long years.

CHAPTER 7

THE GATHERING STORM

Ethan Amador propelled his wheelchair from one side of the vast music room to the other with hands as powerful and sure as they had ever been.

Staring down upon their father from an upper gallery that morning, his sons were sharply aware that despite seeming to have failed dramatically over the past uncertain week, the old man today appeared back to peak physical strength and bristling with anger.

Slash K East had ears every place. It was still short of midday but the spread had already learned of last night's turbulent events resulting in one K West gunhand in hospital and rumours of violence out at that outfit. All this coinciding with the imminent arrival of the overdue beef agent from the south.

How much, or how little of this may have set the old man off on one of his energy tantrums in his big black wheelchair, nobody knew.

With Ethan Amador it was not always possible to identify what might set him off. But today was different for the two towering figures watching from the landing above.

The Amador brothers had weighty matters on their minds that morning, and yet there was actual pleasure in their powerful faces as they watched this once-feared figure whirling about in aimless rage, roaring angrily every so often for his sons.

'Weird,' growled Rod. 'We waited years for him to slip finally over the edge, yet the day he looks like doing it, we've got more on our minds than ever before. Don't you reckon that's crazy?'

'Damned if I do. And damned if I feel I've got any more than usual on my mind.'

'You reckon he might screw things up?' Rod pondered.

'Who knows? I guess I can't figure him any more, the more loco he acts the harder it is to know how he'll be from one day to the next.'

His brother nodded.

It seemed to both that every day now they were seeing increasing signs that the man who'd dominated them with such brutality and power all their lives was undergoing more erratic changes and showing inconsistency in the way he'd reacted to the return of Floyd Ketchell.

Ethan's original plan for that troublemaker was for them simply to stay put here at headquarters and just wait in ambush for when Ketchell would finally feel forced to come out here to seek his revenge. That had plainly failed. They'd quickly realized the former hand turned gunslinger wasn't going to fall into that trap. And yet the old man continued to reject all suggestions of massing the entire ranch crew and going in there after Ketchell – have it over and done with once and for all.

And now the Tumbrille deal. What if he fouled this up? The Paradise contract would fall into their sister's lap like a ripe plum!

It was only recently that Rod had suddenly sensed that the grim truth could be that this man they had justly feared all their lives, had succumbed to fear himself – the fear that came to all with age.

Sure, he still had his days when he could scare a man, when he was genuinely dangerous. But they did not last, were growing less frequent . . . while they had to hold back and maybe even see their sister grab the big prize.

That couldn't be let happen!

But surely today was a day fairly humming with uncertainty.

K East was desperate to secure the Paradise contract and Tumbrille was due there today to talk business. The agent and the old man had never gotten along, but today must be different. So much depended upon that. Yet thus far all they'd heard from Ethan was venom and vitriol directed at the agent, who in reality held the future prosperity of K East in his hand.

Surely this was loco?

Rod Amador knew it.

'He's going to screw it up,' he muttered, massaging heavy biceps, iron jaw sinews rippling under bronzed skin. 'I can feel it, smell it, goddamn taste it.'

His brother nodded. 'Look at the crazy old bastard. He'll give himself a heart attack doing that some day.'

'I've never seen him this bad. . . .' Rod seemed to be thinking out loud. Then he stiffened sharply, ambushed by a thought. 'Damnit, I wonder. . . .'

'What?'

Rod stared fixedly at his brother. 'All this bluff and bluster about drawing Ketchell out here so we can kill the bastard. You don't reckon . . . that maybe that guntipper's got him *scared* to go to town, do you?'

Earl was shocked. But only for a moment. He leaned forward over the railing to watch the wheel-chair jerk to a halt out on the landing. Their father sat there, staring off in the direction of the town with an absent, distracted expression working his features.

Did he seem kind of loco?

He swallowed. This was one hell of a thought to strike a man.

'What do *you* reckon! he countered.

They traded stares. They were big confident men in their late twenties who'd been denied power and authority for too long. The Paradise deal could ensure the ranch's future while a failure would almost certainly see the big contract go to their estranged sister. And for what reason? Simply because the old man no longer seemed capable of good judgement or decision-making any longer.

They believed Ethan had shown poor judgement in not massing the crew and hunting Ketchell down and killing him like a mad dog as soon as he showed, as they certainly would if in charge.

They could live with that.

But business success meant survival, even for a spread their size. The sudden fear that Ethan might screw up the deal with his temper tantrums and attitude just simply wouldn't go away.

Earl straightened soberly as the chair again hummed away beneath them. 'He's sweating some again. Didn't that undertaker posing as a doctor in town tell us once he shouldn't get overheated at his age?'

'Uh-huh. Said it could bring on a heart attack. Or maybe even a stroke – that's what he said.'

A thoughtful silence claimed both men. Heart attack or stroke! Suddenly that sounded almost appealing. The rupture of an aeortic valve or a monstrous cerebral explosion could lead to them ruling here like feudal lords. They dwelt on that possibility. They had never yet been able to envision Ethan nailed down tight in an outsized pine box no matter what his age or the worsening state of his health. Until now?

The chair halted abruptly directly below them and a housemaid appeared smartly to swab Amador's flushed face with a soft towel. He brushed the woman aside and his body language told the sons it was now safe to approach.

'How come everybody his age is in the ground

and he ain't?' Rod complained as they headed downstairs. He was rarely this outspoken but reality seemed to be knocking at the door.

They were disturbed by the news coming out of K West overnight. They were still not sure what had transpired over there apart from the gunhand wounded . . . and possibly some kind of face-down between Jubal Ralls and Floyd Ketchell.

It was this that had triggered off Ethan's tantrum. For Tara's hiring of the Ralls bunch a month earlier was seen by K East as a naked act of defiance and had proven the final straw in the tenuous relationship between father, daughter and youngest son.

It seemed certain blood had been shed on K West, yet paradoxically it also appeared some kind of peace may have been struck in the wake of the gunplay.

That rumour had set the old man off, imagining Tara, son Johnny, Ralls and now Ketchell, all maybe linking up together and likely plotting against himself as the common enemy.

They thought he'd have forgotten this by now, but his first words proved otherwise.

Before they reached his side he was announcing that just as soon as Tumbrille's visit was behind them and contracts exchanged, K East would muster every hand and hired gun to ride into town and squash Ketchell like the insect he was with the most reliable weapons of all: might and power.

He didn't solicit their opinion. He never did. The brothers' faces were a study as they watched him go hurtling away across the imported carpet.

126

'He'll end up getting us strung up before he's through,' Earl said bitterly, massaging his brute jaw. 'We can't hit a whole freaking town! The sheriff hates our guts as it is, and there's no way the county marshal would let us get away with it. There's got to be a dozen simple ways to get rid of one lousy guntipper that won't risk the whole damned county coming down on top of us.'

'It's all right for him.' Rod brooded. 'His life is as good as over . . . has been ever since the day they threw him into that chair. But the day we lay him in the ground is the day we get all that's been coming to us, what we've sweated our guts out for. . . .'

The brothers were silent for a long time. It was not until the father reappeared, bawling orders and causing the fine glassware to tremble on the teak-wood shelves that both seemed struck by the same idea simultaneously.

Suddenly eyes lit up with sinister inspiration. Of course! To save the old bastard from destroying them with his madness, destroy him first!

Yet before they could fully explore this violent inspiration, Ethan erupted into another tantrum and started in cursing them and threatening actual violence as he'd done all their lives.

Slowly the light of inspiration faded from their faces.

They were big, powerful and ambitious men. Yet at times like this they felt more like children who lived in fear of a man who was old, crippled and surely fast going loco. They might pray for his death, but they would never find the courage to kill him.

There had to be another way.

He was a stout man with a ruddy, healthy complexion, quick brown eyes that missed nothing and impressive tong-curled moustaches which were his greatest vanity. He also possessed a sharp and intuitive eye for a good commercial deal and was the most astute beef-buying agent in two hundred miles.

Tom Tumbrille arrived with assistant Conway Royal on the mid-morning stage from Kettle Drum. Never one to waste either time or company money, he checked into the Lucky Strike Hotel and was out on Slash K East's verdant acres checking out their stock by one o'clock.

The men spent two hours out on the range in the company of the brothers Amador while their father followed their movements through field glasses from the mansion.

In that time they inspected stock, pastures, water and dipping facilities. They discussed prices, shipping possibilities, restocking methods and all other matters relevant to the supply of a large number of beeves over a lengthy period of time.

Hawk-eyed Tumbrille was impressed with everything he saw, and that covered not merely the beef cattle side of things. He also carefully noted the numbers, type and disposition of the exceptionally large ranch crew, many of whom appeared to him as if they might well be more adept at punching .45 shells into six-shooters, than punching cows.

Following the inspection, they were treated to a

lavish luncheon at the mansion. The fare was first-rate, the service impeccable. Yet Tumbrille's natural geniality was fading fast when their host began telling him – not asking – what sort of price he would have to pay, the arrangements for shipping, and a dozen other aspects of a contract of this size.

Tumbrille had never cared for Amador whom he found had deteriorated alarmingly since their last testy meeting. He could not conceal his irritation and soon the pair were involved in a slanging match which resulted in Tumbrille driving off in a cloud of dust with no contract proffered or signed.

The brothers were horrified. They attempted to reason with Ethan but he went off in a rage, leaving them staring at one another The brothers sat staring at one another in stony silence. They could picture the contract slipping through their fingers and falling into their sister's lap. It was like the very earth was slipping beneath their feet.

That was the moment when they were finally angry and desperate enough to step out from beneath the old man's huge shadow.

Tara entered the front room, smiling. The tension was thick enough to slice thin. She placed the loaded plates upon the cloth-covered table then stood back with arms folded to watch.

Neither man made a move to begin eating. Ralls hunched his shoulders and tilted his chair back while Ketchell actually took out the makings and began fashioning a cigarette from tobacco and paper.

'All right,' Tara snapped in her bossy way. 'That will be enough of that. Eat, or you may both leave. I mean leave the house and the spread. I have enough on my mind without having to deal with two pig-headed—'

'OK, OK,' Ketchell said, replacing his tobacco in its string bag. He grabbed up knife and fork. 'Look, I'm eating.'

'Me too.' Ralls forced a smile. 'Better join us, Tara. We might get to fighting over the coffee if you don't.'

It was an attempt at humour which helped ease the tension some. And once Tara took her place at table, the conversation flowed easily enough.

Under normal circumstances the violent events of the night before would have dominated, but there was nothing normal about today on K West Ranch. The cattle buyer was on his way and this dominated conversation to such an extent that young Johnny Amador soon grew bored and rose to take down his hat.

Glancing back at his sister as he went to the door, the tall youth was smiling. To his thinking, Floyd Ketchell and Jubal Ralls were about the most impressive and dangerous men he'd ever seen. It made him realize just how smart and grown-up his sister must be to be able to make such a pair toe the line. But then, Sis had always been that way; clever, strong and reliable. About as different from the rest of the Amador family as you could get.

Setting his hat on his head and ambling for the stables, the youth glanced off eastward in the direction of K East. Whenever he thought of his father and brothers, he wondered, half-seriously, if they could all really be of the same blood.

He'd hated the old man from infancy, had come to detest Earl and Rod deeply over the years since. Didn't trust them either. But then, who did?

As he rode off south with the intention of visiting his girl, he saw dust rising above the trees where the town trail wound down. He guessed that would be the cattle buyer. He could leave him to Sis with confidence. If Tara could handle a pair like Ralls, who he didn't like, and Floyd, whom he liked a lot, then managing one fat beef agent should be child's play.

CHAPTER 8

KIDNAPPED

From the upper slopes of tree-clothed Coyote Hill, the K West headquarters was an indistinct jumble of barns, horse yards, house and outbuildings. But the field glasses in Rod Amador's hands brought every-thing jumping close into sharp focus, so much so that he could actually make out the beef agent's big cheesy grin as he stood by his rig chatting with their sister. After a moment the pair shook hands – for about the third time since emerging from the house – and the big man lowered the glasses with a savage curse.

'Every picture tells a stinking story,' he said bitterly. 'Here, take a look.'

Earl Amador's stony features face rarely showed emotion or even expression. But the anger that lit his eyes in that moment was stark, almost frighten-ing.

'Everything down the drain!' he hissed through

clenched teeth, lowering the instrument. 'Look! Now they're shaking hands again! Sweet Judas! We knew this was going to happen just by the way Tumbrille looked when he was quitting K East. That crazy old bastard did it again. He blew our chances clean out the window with his blabbing mouth and his goddamn stiff-necked—'

He broke off sharply, clamping his jaws shut with an act of will. He was not an emotional man, yet he could not quite control himself until he'd inhaled deeply and taken three deep breaths. He lifted his gaze to fasten upon his brother.

'Look me in the eye!' he said quietly.

His anger was under control now, the way it must be if they were to succeed in what he was already planning in order to counteract the reality of what they were seeing far below. His head was buzzing. He knew he was contemplating what could prove to be the most dangerous play of their lives. In the past the brothers had fought Indians, rustlers and horse thieves together, had even committed crimes in the name of K East. Yet always under the command of their father. But blooded in violence and untroubled by conscience, their long-time dream was always to rule the ranch one day and assume the roles of the county's richest and most powerful citizens. Just the two of them.

That day had always been someplace in the hazy future until now. For weeks they had watched the old man slowly coming apart before their eyes in the face of the threat posed by Ketchell.

It showed the stuff they were made of when they

recovered from that shock and began making their own plans. Almost calmly they corkscrewed the stopper out of a fifth of imported whiskey and almost calmly reviewed the startling new challenge facing them and how to deal with it.

In contrast to the interminably slow years they'd spent waiting for this day to arrive at last, they seemed now to slip into their new assertive roles lightning fast. They parleyed and did not let up until they were finally satisfied they had the plan of action they were seeking.

Hit hard and fast was the key.

They must turn the tables on Tara and win back that Paradise contract before Tumbrille quit town.

It would not be easy.

Maybe it would even prove beyond them.

There was only one way to find out and that was by putting the plan into action.

They kept reminding one another they had been waiting for this day all their lives. Now all they must do was stay strong and committed and all they'd ever craved would finally be *theirs*.

Dusk was falling as the brothers sat their horses at the edge of a blackthorn thicket five hundred feet above their sister's home acres.

They had been concealed there an hour watching all the activity down at the headquarters. Until Rod Amador finally grunted, 'Pay dirt at last, I'm thinking. Look.'

'OK, I'm looking, man,' Earl said, squinting. 'What?'

'Yonder.' Rod's gesture encompassed the scene below. 'That skinny rider there is the kid setting off south from the stables, see? At this time of evening he mostly makes for the Ryder place to visit with his girl. We can cut him off easy – but only if we're sure we're ready to go through with what we planned. So . . . are we?'

'We sure as hell are. It's the only way to lock Tara out of the Paradise thing for sure and certain. When she figures it out that she can either drop out of the deal with Tumbrille, or forget about ever seeing Johnny alive again, she's gonna have no choice but to knuckle under and hand us that contract on a platter. . . .'

His voice faded. His brother shot him a quick look. 'What?'

'Just had a flash thought about those two fast guns.'

'Ketchell and Ralls? What about them?'

'They're both stuck on Sis – they both reckon they are almost too fast and flash to die. I'm thinking that after we do what we've come to do, could be we'll see them go hunting the kid and—'

'Think I haven't thought of that?' Rod palmed an envelope from a jacket pocket. 'This is for Tara. I got Joey to write it so she wouldn't recognize the writing. I warned her plain that if Ralls or Ketchell makes one move to go search for the kid afterwards, we'll cut his freaking head off!'

Earl stared at the other. Then he half-smiled. Next he laughed and slapped the saddle horn.

'Hot damn! Always knew you had a head on your

shoulders, bro. That should hobble them tight to her skirts.'

'Not should – will. Think about it, man. Those two hate one another's guts, both sweet on Sis, yet she keeps them apart, even after that dust-up between them the other night. . . .'

He paused with a bemused frown.

'You know, man, it beats me how a woman who weighs no more than a hundred pounds can lead a pair of guntippers around like she's got rings through their noses—'

'Cut the jawbone and get back to what we gotta do!' Earl almost snapped, revealing they were far more tense and edgy than either wanted to admit. For this, at last, was the moment of truth. Win big or risk losing all!

'OK, just take it easy. But we've gotta cover everything. You can rest assured Tara'll be a basket case after Johnny disappears, and we shouldn't have to worry about her fancy men. So that only leaves the old man. OK, we know he's already beginning to come apart before our eyes on account he's scared of Ketchell. But remember, he's always been soft about the kid even though he'd choke on horse droppings rather than own to it. So, when we convince him the "kidnappers" will kill Johnny unless he hands control over to you and me, he's going to go loco and want to take over the manhunt. . . .'

He paused. His brother swore. 'Well, finish what you were saying!'

'He'll *say* that. But then he's gonna remember

something we've known all along. Namely that he's been too yellow scared to leave the house ever since Ketchell showed. So, he'll still be scared, in which case we're going to be free to run the whole play our way. For you and me are going to save both Johnny and K East – after Sis is forced to break off the deal with Tumbrille and the Paradise. We'll be the goddamn heroes of the county and the top dogs on K East. Can't you see it, man?'

Wordlessly, emotionally, big Rod reached out and each man grasped the forearm of the other in their own powerful and almost painful bonding grip. Eyes met and locked and the die was cast.

Side by side they swung their horses back onto the Indian trail leading down to the valley.

He was in the cool gloom of the stables when a slender shadow fell through the doorway. His hand filled with gun swifter than the eye could follow. He grunted when he saw who it was and slipped the weapon away. But she had seen his reaction, and the smile she had brought with her was gone without a trace as she entered to lean against a stack of straw bales.

'Some things never change, do they, Floyd?'

He shrugged.

'You could've been someone else.'

'I've just sent Ralls off to the North Forty to tally the beeves in case Mr Tumbrille wants more facts and figures.'

'Reckon that dealer man lives on facts and figures. But anyway, that's a good sign. He as good as said you'd won the contract before he left. Can't see him considering K East after the way the old man riled him up.'

She studied him with level eyes.

'Do you still intend murdering my father, Floyd?' she asked calmly, too calmly, maybe.

He shrugged.

'And what is that?' she demanded. 'A yes or no?'

He'd not yet told her of his life-changing high drama featuring himself and the man he'd waited five years to kill, played out beneath a weeping sky.

But meeting that level gaze now he realized it was time. He would reveal it all. His blood oath of revenge, the years spent preparing for it, the shock of meeting her again . . . the indecision, uncertainty and finally the resolution.

For a time the only sound in the quiet room was his voice. He sounded unemotional, almost indifferent, and yet had never felt so close to the edge in his life, building a wall between them that nothing could breach.

Then he was drawing to the end. 'I tried to kill him but I couldn't do it,' he admitted. 'It could have been you, it could have been a dozen things. But I knew – I'll always know – that it's over. Your father won't live forever, but however long it might be, he'll never have anything to fear from me.' He paused, studying her pale features. He shrugged, spread his hands. 'That's it . . . just couldn't do it.'

She drew nearer, her expression changing

dramatically in a moment.

'I knew you couldn't,' she said. 'The first day I saw you, I knew that.'

He dropped his eyes. He'd lived with but one purpose for five long years. A man didn't get to wipe that overnight and not leave a yawning gap in his life.

And yet he believed powerfully that this dramatic resolution of his obsession had totally altered the course of his life and left him a different man. Free, liberated and at peace. Or so he hoped.

She came into his arms. 'Floyd, I love you so. I always did, but until now we couldn't—'

'Just a second, Tara. What about Ralls? He's loco about you, and don't tell me that ain't so.' He gestured. 'He sees himself as your protector and right-hand man. And even though I hate to say it, he could prove out to be far better at all that than me. I don't like the man but maybe he's the one you should—'

'He's just a killer,' she said sharply. 'Sure, he's all the things you say too. But Jubal rules with a gun in his hand, and wants to rule me too. I give him room to move and I suppose I've led him on. But that was simply because I needed a strong man about the place and probably shall for a long time, or at least until all this family feuding and bitterness is resolved. But you're the only man I could ever love, Floyd – somehow I managed to go on loving you even when I knew the real reason you'd come back. And now you've changed, Floyd . . . more like the boy I fell in love with. Why are you staring at me that way?'

He was staring because he could scarce believe what she was saying, yet desperately hoped every word was true.

Yet he hesitated in responding when she stood on tiptoe to kiss his cheek. That dramatic night on K East that had brought about the final realization he could not kill the old man, had left him feeling husked out by the knowledge he had wasted five years of his life on an all-consuming hatred which had finally blown away on the wind, leaving him a man without a star.

He couldn't yet envision a future without a driving goal. Couldn't figure what he might become, whether he would work or wander or maybe just sit around in saloons telling yarns about his gunslinger days to other misfits like himself.

Yet when he finally raised his eyes to hers it seemed everything came clear. He bent his head to kiss her on the mouth, then lifted his head sharply when they heard the sound of boots on gravel outside. Running boots.

It was Ralls. The gunman was breathless and held a slip of paper in his fingers as he lunged in.

'Tara,' he panted. 'Coley just found this tied to a brick on the title gate. It's . . . it's for you. . . !'

She snatched it and scanned the hand-written lines. All colour drained from her face and Ketchell was forced to support her. He grabbed the paper and held it up to the dim light.

Scrawled by a leaden bullet, the note read:

We've got Johnny. Don 't go to the law and don't talk to anybody until we contact you again or you'll get him back in a box.

CHAPTER 9

BADLAND GUNS

He rode steadily as night drew a dark cloak about him. But when a crescent moon tilted its horn and spilled a pale light across the gaunt-ribbed badlands, Ketchell kicked the hammerhead into a trot and moved directly into the soft yellow glow.

The horse shook its head wearily but did not falter. The rider rolled a smoke one-handed and set it alight with the sweep of a lucifer. His narrowed eyes probed restlessly for sign in some of the ugliest country in the territory. But there was not a single print, no broken twig or a pile of dung to indicate that the hunch he was playing might be the right one.

Yet he pressed on.

Back in the old days the Damaron badlands had been a fine place to escape to with your young buddies, where you could escape hard work and responsibility and just go skylarking around in the barren wilderness, or maybe hunt wolf or cougar to the heart's content.

Familiar stone landmarks loomed up and drifted by in this strange badlands light like ghostly Indian totems. Yet his attention remained focused upon the dull, rust-hued earth he was crossing, mile after endless mile. He cut the tracks of horses and wild critters but all were old and of no value. With no clear notion how many had been involved in young Johnny Amador's abduction, he would settle for just a single fresh hoof print at this stage. Anything.

Back on the Bolte family's B.B. spread where the kid had gone missing, nobody had seen or heard anything unusual after the boy had drifted off looking to bag a quail hen for his girlfriend's supper, before failing to return.

Ketchell was just playing a hunch, combing the badlands. But he was prepared to follow it through, still saw it as the strongest chance.

His brain was beginning to feel dull and sluggish by the time another fruitless mile drifted behind. His knees grew thick with fatigue and his shirt clung to his scarred back with sweat.

He frowned and squinted across at some small white object in the sand in the middle distance over by a ghost-grey deadfall. He was riding on when something clicked in his tired brain prompting him to rein in sharply and turn back.

It was a cigarette butt.

Jumping to ground he began searching the immediate area with renewed energy. He scouted out from the deadfall in ever-widening circles until he came upon the spot where a profusion of fresh sign showed where men and riders had recently spelled up before striking off on a due east by south-east course.

Three men and three horses. The smallest set of prints were those of Johnny Amador, showing the kid was still alive at this point. The others were made by high-heeled cowboy boots, the type favoured by ranch hands.

Quick and alert again by this, he set about covering the surrounds at a jog-trot without pause until something else that didn't fit naturally into this barren landscape attracted his quick eye. He bent from the waist to scoop up a half-smoked cigar butt, this time. It was the Amarillo brand, a damned fine cigar and expensive, with a distinctive aroma.

He clearly recalled a K East bronco buster named Flynn passing round a box of that brand of fat Cubans the first night he'd encountered the Amador brothers in Flintlock.

He stood motionless, features taking on the wolf-look of the hunter with a fresh scent.

K East?

The ranch had been high on his suspicion list from the outset, as it had to be. But this was the first tangible clue to point the Amadors' way.

Yet he needed to be sure.

The old man, he mused? No. He couldn't see that. The once all-powerful patriarch of K East had already shown he was afraid to quit the security of the house a dozen times over recent weeks. Rod and Earl? Could be. But why?

He was beginning to sweat, though the night was

chill. Maybe he was loco imagining that even that cold-blooded breed would commit such a crime against their own flesh and blood.

Suddenly he swung about and went jogging back to the spot where the kidnappers' sign gave out at the edge of the limestone trace. He'd examined the prints before but concentrated far more intensely on them now.

At length he straightened and blew a gust of breath through his teeth, convinced it was K East horses that had gone through here.

His expression turned cold and hard. The impulse was to run back to the horse and get riding. He resisted it. Two hundred yards from the sandy shale, the kidnappers had deliberately set their mounts across a vast shelf of limestone which, as he'd already seen, left no marks.

This meant his quarry could have struck off in any direction of the compass; he could hunt for sign out there on the limestone all day and come up with nothing. So he rolled a smoke and hunkered down to do some thinking. Roughly ten miles east of where he was, ran a series of deep arroyos which boasted good ground water, a rarity in the badlands. If he was a kidnapper on the run in this dry and hostile country, that would be the direction he would take.

He swung up into the saddle and touched the horse with spur.

Trailing cigarette smoke he rode at a lope wearing a frown. Why would the Amadors abduct their own brother? It didn't make sense. There must be a simpler explanation, even if he couldn't come up with one.

He pushed the horse harder. It jerked its head back, trying to bite his knee. He paid no attention. Some miles further along he glimpsed in far distance the lonesome shack perched on the side of a hill that was the house of the hermit hide-hunter, Juan Escobar.

He wondered if Juan had seen or heard anything, but couldn't stop by to find out. He must stick to his hunch, knowing every minute could prove vital.

As he rode into the first arroyo he reached an hour later, he caught the whiff of wood smoke.

Bellying up behind a sickly spruce, he slumped low on hearing a murmur of voices. A stone's throw ahead was the glow of a campfire. Crawling closer, he sighted Johnny trussed up sitting with his back against a boulder. A hardcase towner named Matt Flynn stood before the boy, talking to him.

Focusing on the boy's strained face, Ketchell felt his rage rise. The .38 was already in his fist, cocked and ready. He searched for sign of the Amadors but could only glimpse another roughneck from Liberty, a bum named Mears.

With wolf stealth he began circling the campsite, belly-wriggling through red sand. He was looking for the Amadors, yet sensed they must be gone; men that size found it hard to make themselves invisible. He continued onwards, not fully realizing until almost too late that he was over-exhausted and too angry to show proper caution.

He lifted his head above a boulder and looked across at the bound boy. A short distance away a third roughneck named Wallace was dipping water from the little creek. The man was staring directly straight at him.

'Ketchell!'

The shout shattered the stillness and the towner went diving for cover clawing at the gun on his hip as Ketchell swung up his Colt and triggered.

He didn't miss. Wallace threw up his gun and went down in a way that said he would never get up.

Johnny turned and shouted a warning to him. As Flynn opened up from cover, Ketchell glimpsed the third man dashing for the half-hidden horses.

And still no sign of the Amadors.

He tried for a stopping shot as Mears changed position. The runner was hit, but wild-eyed and loco-looking in the thin moonlight, he touched off a shot that passed by Ketchell's face so close that he felt the heat of its passage. He dropped lower, adjusted his aim and drilled the man through the chest dead centre.

They had the numbers but not the edge. For this was not a battle between equals but lethal gunfighter versus town scum more suited to beating up women or kidnapping boys than fighting for their lives.

Ketchell sprang upright and and took off fast in the direction where the third man had vanished. He heard a hoarse shout followed by the rapid stutter of hoofs on rock before he'd crested a swell. He ducked low then hurled his body full length as a mounted Flynn let fly with three wild shots before throwing himself low over the animal's neck. He raked viciously with rowel spurs and horse and rider shot away to be engulfed in a towering wall of deep brush.

Unscathed yet blowing hard, Ketchell was cursing himself for his recklessness when he heard, 'Floyd? Is that you, Floyd?'

The kid was unharmed. He saw that the moment he leapt to his feet and ran towards him. He thanked God, something he had not done in five godless years.

The old man wheeled his chair through the doors then hit the brakes hard with his hand lever. He was angry yet confused, visibly so.

'What the tarnal is all this uproar about?' he roared. 'You fools, don't you know what time it is?'

The brothers turned away from a dust-coated Matt Flynn to stare blankly at their father. They appeared strange, so the old man thought, almost menacing. Yet nobody menaced the master of K East – or so he had always believed. But that was in the past as the recent weeks that had seen the new guard take over on Slash K East. Although full of brag and bluster, Ethan Amador had revealed himself as a spent force when he'd failed to lead them in the conflict with Floyd Ketchell. Deep down he suspected the change, but was ready to reassert his authority right at that moment. He opened his mouth to begin shouting, then found himself incapable of speech when Rod suddenly loomed before him.

But was this his son Rod or some total stranger?

Blinking upwards, old Ethan Amador realized he was staring into the stone face of the biggest and most dangerous man he'd ever seen. And in that same moment, at last saw the reality and the truth. It had been a long time coming, but this was the day the old man's two first-born had finally exploded free from a lifetime of suppression and intimidation imposed by him. And the transition was complete.

They were no longer either fearful or subservient, could never be so again. They had evolved into something truly chilling – replicas of himself.

'Get the hell out of my sight, old man! We're talking business. You heard me. Get!'

For one final moment the still powerful old man appeared almost dangerous, inflating his huge chest and glaring with all the old ferocity. Yet with the son still menacing him at close quarters, staring that way, there came the moment when it felt as though something had impaled his great body – some jagged lightning stroke of fear and final understanding that went through him and left him shaking.

He saw they were still his flesh and blood. But they were now giants, as he had once been but would never be again. Their eyes and faces were murderous and arrogant as he had been for so long, but never would be again.

His destruction was complete.

Wordlessly, Earl Amador reached out and spun

the wheelchair round with one big forefinger. Then he deliberately drove his knee into the back of the unit which shot away to crash into a chair, breaking it apart. With fumbling hands the blabby old man straightened the wheels and guided it clumsily off through the closest doorway, not daring to look back.

His era was over. And staring bleakly at the haggard Flynn, Rod Amador still believed his own long-awaited time had come. But knew, in view of what the rider had just reported, that this time could prove short-lived if they didn't act fast. He had taken a huge risk in his attempt to force his sister out of the vital struggle for the Paradise contract. The abduction of his kid brother as a hostage had gone well – until suddenly it had gone all wrong, because of just one man.

Ketchell.

'That stinking gunslick will cart Johnny into town and go blab to the goddamn law!' he roared – just like the old man. 'But he won't live to brag about it.' He lunged for the doors. 'Come on, we're riding!'

CHAPTER 10

THE LAST GUNDOWN

It was to be a night like no other.

From the moment the staggering down-and-out lurched into Upper Main Street by the fire station, bawling for the sheriff in the early morning hours, Liberty was being jarred awake, soon to be alarmed, and finally gripped by a kind of terror.

The sheriff heard the shouting, but rolled over on his hard cot at the lawhouse and tugged the blanket up around his leathery neck. Damned drunks! Prohibition would be a damn good thing! He was dozing again . . . almost off.

But then the hysterical voice right outside the law office:

'There's a whole bunch of fellers packing guns making for the Five-Dollar Roomer, Sheriff!'

The sheriff's bare feet hit the floor with a thud. Two blocks away, someone with powerful lungs was running down the wide main stem, shouting, 'Mr Ketchell – Floyd! Look out, they's coming to get you, Mr Ketchell!'

Liberty was no longer pretending to be asleep after that. Lights flickered on and faces peered blearily from windows. Then the first citizen staggered out his door into the main stem, hitching up his braces and squinting about to see what all the racket was about.

When he sighted men with guns he tried to get back inside again but the press of curious people following him out made it impossible.

All this sounded exciting – they thought.

By the time Tara Amador's party from Slash K West appeared around the Hobbs Street corner with a rig flanked by five riders, the sheriff was standing out in the centre of Main waving a Colt and calling on the fast-swelling crowd to settle down, punctuating his orders with a shot into the sky. Close by, the the man who'd first raised the alarm stood staring out at all the excitement, eyes rolling, scared yet impressed by what he'd started off.

The man saw a chance to be of further 'help' when Tara Amador jumped down from her rig, followed by her youngest brother – the one whom all the fuss had been about. The young man was plainly unhurt and appeared totally recovered from his ordeal.

On unsteady skinny legs, the red-nosed drunk weaved his way forward through the milling crowd as the K West party encircled the buckboard, when one of the mounted escorts astride a flash horse bumped him deliberately and sent him flying. He hit the ground and rolled, got up on one knee to blink up at the towering figure of Jubal Ralls.

'W-what did you do that for, boy—?'

'Keep back, old man!'

Ralls swung his horse in a circle to drive back the curious ones first, then sprang lithely to ground and handed the reins to a cowboy. The gunman went directly to Tara's side. 'Stay close to me!' he ordered, brandishing his Colt now. 'Make space, damnit. Back up.' Then, 'So what the hell is going on?'

Nobody seemed sure – for a moment. Then a weathered oldster thrust to the fore, waving his hands and was forced to shout to make himself heard.

'Ain't it the Five Dollar Roomer where young Ketchell's lodgin', Miss Tara? Well, anyways, that's where them geezers with guns was heading.' He reached as high as he could stretch. 'Huge . . . a couple of them . . . timbertops!'

Tara whirled to Ralls. 'It must be my brothers!' she cried. 'Are we too late?'

'Too late for what?' the gunfighter replied. 'Look, we headed in here to roust out the sheriff and charge your brothers with—'

He broke off as the girl whirled and vanished in the surging mob. Ralls cursed, hesitated just a moment, then swapped alarmed stares with Johnny as a gunshot's crash ripped through the clamour.

C'mon!' the boy yelled, and side by side they

went ploughing through the press of bodies, ignoring a hoarse shout from the sheriff demanding to know what in hell was going on.

The K West party found two Amadors and three ranch-hands emerging from the roomer, cursing and shouting orders. But there was no sign of Floyd Ketchell.

It felt strangely peaceful sitting there upon the broken fence with the dark shape of the juniper tree whispering in the night above him.

Serene.

He dragged deeply on his cigarette and the brief red glow tinted his features and was mirrored in his eyes.

He wondered, in a strangely remote and detached kind of way, if there could be another spot in Liberty right at that moment halfway as peaceful as this.

He doubted it.

He'd found the entire town asleep beneath a high-riding moon upon his return. He'd intended to roust Yearly out of his blankets upon his arrival in order to lay charges against the Amadors. Yet something had steered him here first. He realized now he'd desperately needed to draw breath and relax, however briefly, before what could easily evolve into a head-on showdown with the K East.

But maybe he'd stayed here too long?

He shrugged off the last of his earlier exhaustion and rose to his feet just as the first streak of pink appeared in the east. Judging by the clamour reaching him from Main, he figured the Amadors might well have come to town. He'd not been sure if the clan would fold up or fight, following their failed kidnap attempt. Maybe he should have realized they might choose the latter course. They had always treated the law with contempt, for the law here was still but one sheriff and a couple of seedy deputies. He had no reason to believe the Amadors would be concerned about the law if they had come here with men and guns. Almost certainly they would be coming after him with the intention of silencing him before he could run to the law with evidence of their crime. They would be after blood tonight. His blood.

It was not too late to fork leather and ride, if he was of a mind. But he had known all along he would stay and see it through. Would – and must.

For looking back, he must admit that it had been himself, Floyd Ketchell, who had initially set the flame to the tinder here. He'd vanished for five years, returned out of no place with a gun and a look that would have convinced even the town fool why he was back.

Everything that had ensued evolved from that.

Yet having conceded that, he believed and always would, that he was right and the Amador clan wrong. No free man should have had to endure what he had suffered. He'd come back to mete out the justice the law had failed to provide for him.

He'd partially succeeded in this, but now conceded it was he who'd stirred up old emotions and hatreds and maybe driven the Amadors to over-play their raging hand.

A man simply could not touch off a fire that way then ride off when it erupted into a blaze.

'Real philosophical, gunfighter,' he half-smiled as he rose. Then, moving neither fast nor slow, he walked towards the lights.

It was a combination of communal fear and simple self preservation that saw the Main Street mob panic and instantly forsake the wide street for the plankwalks and store walks the moment the slim figure in the yellow hat appeared around Duke's Corner.

The sheriff came rushing forward, waving his arms at Ketchell and shouting – nobody could hear what. Yet Ketchell just shoved Yearly aside and kept coming with that same unhurried walk, like someone who had done this kind of thing before.

Half a block further along, Rod Amador was first to step down off the saloon porch and stood with boots widespread, the dawn wind toying with his silken bandanna.

One by one the others joined him. Suddenly a woman in the crowd cried out, 'Mother of mercy! Are they going to murder that boy?'

While off to one side before the haberdasher's store, hard fingers dug into Tara Amador's arm like the jaws of a vice.

'You're not buying into this, damn!' Ralls hissed. 'He wants to die – so let him. There's a passel of them and just one of him – he's got to be loco!'

'Let me go, Ralls,' Tara cried. 'I can stop him – I will!'

'I tell you he wants to die. Nobody takes on odds like that! He's tired of living, so why should you care?'

'I love him. Can't you see that, you fool?'

Something seemed to go out of handsome Jubal Ralls at that. His face was suddenly grim and pale and sombre as he scanned her tear-stained face, and realized that what she'd said was so. Every feature and shining tear affirmed it.

He grimaced bitterly. Moments earlier he'd been calmly observing the mounting drama and pictured the inevitable outcome. He saw Ketchell dead, Tara dependent on him and his gun, and Slash K East in the worst kind of trouble over the kidnap attempt that might well bring the whole arrogant tribe of them down before they were through.

And her learning to love him.

Only it would not be that way. He saw that now – clearer than he'd ever seen anything. Until he could not bear to see any more of it. . . .

She screamed when he released her arm and jumped down off the plankwalk into the dust. Up ahead, Ketchell turned his head his way, and Ralls quickened his pace.

'Always the grandstander, aren't you, Ketchell? Well, you're not about to grandstand me out of this fool hand you're playing, by God. I keep telling her I'm the better man and I'll prove it or—'

He got no further. In back of the towering Amadors, a jittery K East gunhand lost his nerve and whipped out his Colt revolver. It was a reckless action which could not be reversed. Instantly

Ketchell and Ralls came clear together with such blinding speed that their volley blasted the cowboy backwards off the landing before he could even jerk trigger.

As every enemy hissed from leather, the gun storm broke.

Ralls's first sure shot killed Earl Amador before his Colt was fully clear of leather. Ketchell bobbed low as a bullet whined over his shoulder, straightened and drilled a snarling gunman dead centre.

Then he was hit.

The pain bolted down his left arm and sent him lurching sideways. But almost instantly he realized it was merely a flesh wound. Ducking low defensively, he stared through roiling gunsmoke to glimpse Ralls's fierce grin as the guntipper fanned .45 hammer and a scything hail of bullets pounded a hulking K East gunner clear off the landing with crimson spurting from a line of holes studding his barrel chest.

Through towering moments of gunmanship and bloody uncertainty, the two fast guns stood side by side trading lead with an enemy that boasted superior numbers but far lesser gunskills. Ketchell was already inhaling the first heady whiff of victory when two lightning shots from Ralls smashed into a raging Rod Amador and drove his massive bulk back.

'What a team!' Ralls laughed, then staggered backwards in the same moment as a falling Amador's gun roared like a cannon.

Enraged, unstoppable now, Ketchell sprang up

onto the decking as the wounded giant wheeled drunkenly to retreat. Ketchell pumped three roaring shots into the giant's backbone, saw him fall like a lopped oak, whirled in search of another target only to find there was none. Only moaning and bloodied men – amongst the silent ones – with Sheriff Yearly striding up and down the blood-spattered boards pumping shots into a lightening sky and cowering the survivors with his authority – a real peace officer at last!

But every triumph exacts its cost.

Floyd reached Ralls's side while the man was still breathing.

'Look after her, Ketchell . . . it's you she loves. . . .' He turned his head, searching for her, then was still.

Ketchell rose slowly and stiffly to to turn his back upon the dead and the triumphantly alive alike.

His face was that of an old man as he started to trudge away, blood dripping from his sleeve. Then Tara was there, reaching for him in silence, tears of relief coursing down her cheeks with both grief and love clear in her eyes.

Walking away, arm in arm, and with his discarded gun lying back there some place for some trophy hunter to find, he was at once a man wearied and hurting, yet knew in that instant he felt more hopeful and free than ever before in his life.

But surely there was also something else that was equally dramatic, and different. But what?

He paused. She held him close. Then he smiled and they started off together again when he realized what that feeling of pleasant strangeness really was. For the first time in five long years, the pain in his back had left him.